PIRATES OF POSEIDON

AN ANCIENT GREEK MYSTERY

BLOOMSBURY

Bloomsbury Publishing Plc
50 Bedford Square, London, WC1B 3DP, UK

BLOOMSBURY, BLOOMSBURY EDUCATION and the Diana logo are trademarks of
Bloomsbury Publishing Plc

First published in Great Britain in 2018 by Bloomsbury Publishing Plc

Text copyright © Saviour Pirotta, 2018
Illustrations copyright © Freya Hartas, 2018

Saviour Pirotta and Freya Hartas have asserted their rights under the Copyright, Designs
and Patents Act, 1988, to be identified as Author and Illustrator of this work.

A catalogue record for this book is available from the British Library

ISBN: PB: 978-1-4729-4020-9; ePDF: 978-1-4729-4021-6; ePub: 978-1-4729-4018-6

2 4 6 8 10 9 7 5 3 1

Typeset by Newgen KnowledgeWorks Pvt. Ltd., Chennai, India
Printed and bound in the UK by CPI Group (UK) Ltd, Croydon CR0 4YY

To find out more about our authors and books visit www.bloomsbury.com
and sign up for our newsletters

PIRATES OF POSEIDON

AN ANCIENT GREEK MYSTERY

SAVIOUR PIROTTA

Illustrated by FREYA HARTAS

BLOOMSBURY EDUCATION

LONDON   OXFORD   NEW YORK   NEW DELHI   SYDNEY

For Pauline Thresh and Kirsty Fenn at Leeds School Library Services, and for librarians everywhere. The world would be a much poorer place without them.

CONTENTS

PROLOGUE

The Ship with no Eyes

Late Summer, 433 BC

The warship moved swiftly through the night, a vast shadow propelled by thirty oarsmen who worked in total silence. Its wooden hull was painted jet black to match its one rectangular sail. There was no wind and the sail hung limply against the mast. It had a golden mask painted across it, glaring out over the sea with blank, hollow eyes. The rowers wore masks too, though theirs were black and had small eyeholes through which they could peep.

A small group of hoplites stood at the back of the ship, bristling with spears. The soldiers also wore masks: shiny black ones that made them look like human ants. And they had been trained to fight with the ruthlessness of ants too. Legend had a name for them: myrmidons.

The only sound on board the ship came from the piper sitting at the stern. He was not playing music to soothe the rowers or honour the gods. The short, sharp notes from his aulos helped the rowers work in perfect rhythm.

Toot… toot… toot.

A small lamp flickered at an altar beside him, throwing shadows on a small image of Poseidon, god of the sea. The rest of the ship was shrouded in darkness.

A tall man stood at the prow with his back to the rowers and the hoplites. He was dressed in a thick himation pulled over his head to conceal his face. A second, shorter figure stood next to him. This person also wore a cloak over his head. Its folds fell around his round shoulders making him look like a bloated ghost. On his feet he had expensive boot sandals, cut from the best leather. They were new and creaked as he shifted his weight from one leg to the other.

Earlier, the night had been clear, with bright stars strewn like gold dust across the sky. But now a thick mist rose out of the sea, wrapping the black ship in a ghostly veil that blotted out the stars and hid the coast from view. A worried murmur went through the rowers even as they struggled to keep up with the piper. This part of Hellas was infamous for its hidden reefs. Many a ship had run aground on them, sending its unlucky crew to the bottom of the sea.

A few broke the silence and called out Poseidon's name. 'Oh, god of the sea, protect us. We beg you.'

The tall man in the himation barked out an order. 'Be quiet! Fools.'

He threw a glance at his shorter companion. Unlike the sailors, the tall man considered the mist a sign of good fortune. It was the breath of the dark gods and spirits that lurked under the waves. Those gods were his mentors and guardians. His inspiration. He wrapped his hands around a golden amulet hanging from a chain round his neck, an image of Melinoe, the much-feared goddess of ghosts. It always brought him good luck.

Let my plan succeed, oh sacred dark one, he murmured. *Answer my prayers and I will make you the most revered goddess in the world. I shall build temples for you everywhere.*

The ship's helmsman, the man in charge of the rowers, spoke through the mist. 'I suggest we slow down a little, sir. If memory serves me well, we must be very close to the shore. We don't want to run aground on some hidden rocks.'

The man in the himation answered without turning. 'The gods of the sea will not let us perish. Have faith in the dark ones. And in me. I know these waters like the back of my hand.'

He snapped his fingers at the piper, who tooted faster. The ship gathered speed, some of the rowers crying out in pain as the oars slipped out of their hands.

The tall man nudged his companion. 'Bring a light.'

The shorter fellow carried an unlit torch to Poseidon's altar and returned with it flaming and guttering. The man in the himation took it from him and waved it in a huge arc above his head.

A second light flashed through the mist and the tall man barked an order at the helmsman. 'Tell the men to stop rowing.'

The piper put down his aulos and the warship juddered to a halt.

'There is someone waiting on the shore,' continued the tall man, looking at the hoplites. 'You – go and fetch him. And make sure he has come alone.'

The man waiting on the shore had been there for hours, hidden behind a huge rock. Now he saw a raft approaching through the mist. It had a crew of three, two rowing, one standing to attention with a spear. A hoplite. When it came close to the rocks, the man stepped out of his hiding place.

'Hold up your torch so we can see,' called the hoplite. 'Are you alone?'

The man on the shore did as he was asked, while at the same time patting a small jewelled dagger hidden under his sash. He was glad he'd brought it with him. Pirates were notorious for their quick temper. You never knew when you might need a knife to defend yourself. 'Yes, I came alone. I was warned not to bring anyone with me.'

He was a short man, hugely fat, wrapped in thick layers of multi-coloured silk. His hair was heavily oiled and reflected the light from the torch. Gold rings sparkled on his fingers and hung from his fleshy ears. He waited till the raft touched the rocks, then stepped deftly aboard, carrying his bulk with surprising ease. The hoplite snatched the torch from him and hopped on to the shore. He peered around.

'You will not find anyone hiding behind the rocks,' wheezed the fat man. 'Cyrus the treasure hunter always keeps his word, especially to esteemed pirates such as yourselves.'

The hoplite doused the torch in the sea before climbing back on the raft. He pushed away from the rocks with the back end of his spear and the other two men started rowing again. A coastal breeze had thinned the sea fret and Cyrus could see the warship's immense hull looming above him. All seafaring vessels had eyes painted on the prow, to help them find their way and to scare away storms, but the eyes on this ship had been blacked out.

Cyrus shook his head at the folly of this. Did the captain of this vessel consider himself immune to the anger of the gods and the ocean spirits? A ship without eyes was blind and cursed. It would lead its men to certain death at the bottom of the sea.

Hands reached down from the bulwarks as the raft bumped against the hull. Cyrus let them haul him aboard, careful to avoid the oars, whose sharp blades could crack his skull open like an egg.

Clambering aboard, he thought he heard ghosts wailing deep inside the ship. He shivered and made the sign of the horn with his left hand to ward off evil. Were they the voices of dead sailors? Could this mysterious ship with its blind hull and masked rowers be haunted?

One of two men standing at the prow spoke without turning. 'Welcome, oh finder of lost treasures.'

'I am honoured to be on board your ship,' replied Cyrus, lying through his teeth. Now that his feet were planted firmly on the boards, he could not hear the ghostly voices any more. Perhaps his imagination had played a trick on him.

He turned to the crew. 'A blessed evening to all.' He forced himself to smile, expecting someone to return his greeting. No one spoke. The rowers and hoplites merely stared back at him, their eyes glinting through the peepholes in their masks.

Without warning, the piper started tooting on his aulos. The ship lurched, catching Cyrus off balance. He crashed to the deck, banging his head on the planks.

The ghostly voices rang through Cyrus's head again. He shook it to clear his mind and looked around in alarm. The warship was moving swiftly, heading back out to sea.

The taller of the two men at the prow turned suddenly, revealing a golden mask on his face. Cyrus caught his breath. The man in the golden mask was the most notorious – the most feared – pirate in the Hellenic world. Cyrus gazed into his eyes as if hypnotised, like a mouse caught in a serpent's glare.

The mask was the most exquisite thing he had ever seen. The cheekbones were high, the eyes narrow slits. There was a short curly beard carved along the chin. A crown of shimmering leaves decorated the forehead.

The second figure turned an instant later and Cyrus realised it was a boy. He too wore a mask but his was made of silver. It showed the grinning face of a young Dionysus. The cheeks were chubby, the hair fashioned into thick, unruly curls. The large mouth was open to show a permanent, leery laugh. Cyrus could see the boy's real teeth through it. The front ones were broken.

He struggled to his feet and the pirate in the golden mask came forward.

'Do you have it?'

'Yes. I had to grease many palms, even slash a throat or two, but I have it for you.'

The pirate held out a hand heavy with rings. 'I was told you are the best treasure hunter in the world. That is why I sent one of my men to task you with finding it.'

'And I did.' Cyrus removed a small pouch from under his sash, pulled it open and poured its contents into the pirate's open palm.

The boy in the silver mask brought the torch closer, revealing an intricate necklace hung all over with jingling charms.

Anger flashed in the eyes of the pirate in the golden mask. 'This is not what I wanted, you fool. You have brought the wrong treasure.'

Cyrus opened and closed his mouth like a hooked fish. 'Cyrus the treasure hunter never makes a mistake. Your man must have given me the wrong information.'

'Silence,' roared the pirate in the golden mask. 'I am not interested in how the mistake happened. This bauble is of no use to me.' He turned suddenly and hurled the necklace over the prow.

'This sorry business with our guest from the East is concluded,' he barked at the boy. 'Do with him as you please.'

Sensing these moments could be his last, Cyrus reached for his jewelled dagger. But the boy was too quick for him. He snatched the weapon from under the treasure hunter's sash, ripping the fabric in the process.

'I risked life and limb to keep my side of the bargain,' protested Cyrus, grabbing at the torn sash. 'There are some rules that must be obeyed, even by pirates. I claim the protection of Poseidon and safe passage back to land, as is my right by the laws of the seas.'

The boy roared with laughter. 'Or what? You will report us to the nearest magistrate?'

He leaped at Cyrus again and slashed at the pockets in his robe. A leather purse fell out and moon-white pearls rolled across the deck. Cyrus went down on his hands and knees, trying to retrieve them. But the boy was all around him like a wild beast, kicking, biting, tearing the rings off the treasure hunter's fingers and ears.

'In the name of the gods, have mercy. I am old enough to be your grandfather. Have you no shame?'

Bellowing with laughter, the boy pulled Cyrus up and hurled him over the bulwarks like a bale of straw.

'May Poseidon put an everlasting curse on you. May the monster Charybdis swallow you whole and spit out your bones. The both of you.' The treasure hunter had only time to scream a few words before salt water filled his mouth and the current pulled him under.

The boy hooted with laughter and spat into the sea to reverse the curse. Then he picked up the spilled pearls and returned to the pirate in the golden mask.

The taller man put a hand gently on his shoulder. 'You may keep the fool's possessions. You have earned them.'

The boy thrust the pearls in a bag and slipped the rings on his fingers. He stretched out his hands to admire them. 'Thank you, sir.'

The man in the golden mask turned away and scowled at the sea. He was furious that his plan had gone wrong. Tearing the Melinoe amulet from his neck, he hurled it into water. From now on he would pray to no more gods, not even the dark ones. He would offer no more sacrifice until he had what he wanted. The infamous pirate in the golden mask would rely solely on his own cunning and ruthless ambition.

But one thing was certain. The treasure he desired so badly would one day be his.

CHAPTER ONE

Master Ariston's Play

My friend Thrax was holding up a polished mirror so that our master, Ariston, could admire his reflection. Master Ariston is a travelling poet and a singer. Thrax is his personal slave. He looks after our master's daily needs, like washing his clothes, polishing his boots and making him meals when no professional cooks are available.

I work for Master Ariston too but I am a freeborn scribe. My job is to write down every song and poem that he makes up. They're drivel most of the time but I never complain. I'm lucky to have a secure job. My parents are aging farmers on the island of Kos and they depend on me to send them money.

Master Ariston was gabbling on about the exciting evening ahead. But I could tell Thrax was only half listening. He was also thinking about something else.

Most people can only think properly when they're alone or in a quiet place. I'm one of them. When I'm trying to figure something out, I have to cut myself off from everyone or else I get muddled. The smallest noise can disrupt my thinking. My friend Thrax is very different. He has the ability to think and figure out very complex problems while talking about something completely different.

What was on his mind now, I wondered?

'Master,' he said from behind the mirror. 'It occurred to me…'

'Not now, Thrax,' cut in Master Ariston as he peered closer at his reflection. 'We have to get ready for the play.'

Master Ariston has been a poet all his life but last year in Corinth we met Euripides, one of the most respected playwrights in the world. He inspired Master Ariston to try his hand at playwriting too. So in the spring we travelled to Delphi, where our master consulted the famous oracle to discover if he should ditch poetry in favour of drama and writing comedies.

The oracle always speaks in riddles but her advice this time seemed to be very clear, at least to Master Ariston.

Turning a corner in life, the poet shall come across a sea of merriment.

Master Ariston took that to mean his comedies would meet with great success, so we rented a country house in Delphi where he would have the peace and quiet to write. And now we were back in Corinth at the end of summer, about to attend a reading of Master Ariston's first play – *The Dolphins*. It wasn't going to be a public performance, just a private one for rich people who might want to sponsor the play and help it appear at the great festival in Athens next year.

I want to be a writer too, but a very different kind from Master Ariston. I want to write exciting stories that I can perform at parties, which we call symposiums. I've already got two finished works under my belt. They're mystery stories based on my real-life adventures with Thrax. One is set in Corinth, where we clashed with a dangerous gang of thieves. The second takes place in Delphi. That's where we rescued a girl from two ruthless kidnappers.

Thrax has plans for the future too. He is desperate to buy his freedom so he can return to his home in Thrace. There he hopes to be reunited with his mother, whom he last saw when he was a toddler, before he became a slave. Buying your freedom costs a lot of money, which is why very few slaves manage to do it. Thrax is trying to earn the funds by solving mysteries for rich clients. I'm helping him.

The venue for Master Ariston's comedy debut was a place Thrax and I knew well – the andron in a house that belonged to a wealthy merchant called Zenon the Younger. He is a close friend of Master Ariston's father and we stayed at his house the last time we were in Corinth.

It's where Thrax and I were given our first mystery to solve. It's also the home of our friend Fotini – Zenon's daughter – and her personal slave, Gaia, who helped us with the case. After that they became members of our secret society, the Medusa League, which we set up to solve mysteries for people in trouble.

'Ha,' roared Master Ariston, startling me out of my thoughts. 'I am now ready to face the great and good of Corinth.'

Thrax put down the polished mirror. 'Master, I really…'

'Shush,' tutted Master Ariston. 'You go on like a pesky mosquito, young Thrax. It's a good job I'm a kind man from Athens or I would have your tongue cut out. He patted down his newly oiled hair. 'I must admit, barbers in Corinth are far more talented than the ones in Athens. The onc I visited today is a genius with the scissors. He's managed to make me look just like Euripides the playwright.'

'That barber is nothing but a reckless gambler and a desperate thief,' said Thrax. 'He stole money from right under your nose while you were sitting in his chair.'

Master Ariston scowled. 'A gambler and a thief? I hardly think so. He is the most popular barber in the city. His shop was packed with illustrious clients.'

'Why don't you look in your purse, master?' said Thrax.

Master Ariston did so, and his face fell when he counted out the money. 'The scoundrel! He's a thief all right. Look at that. He's practically cleaned me out.'

'And he's a gambler as I said,' repeated Thrax. 'He's been caught cheating at dice at least twice. That's how he lost two of the fingers on his right hand.'

Master Ariston's lips quivered like a landed carp's. 'How did you know the barber only has three fingers? You didn't come to the barbershop with me. I left you here to get my clothes ready.'

'He left greasy marks on your purse as he robbed you, master. They indicate he has only three fingers. The other two were chopped off as punishment for cheating at the gambling table.'

'Poor fellow,' said Master Thrax as he pulled the strings on his purse to close it. 'The law can be too harsh sometimes.'

'It wasn't the magistrate who ordered the punishment. It was his friends, the other gamblers. That's how they deal with cheats in the gambling world. They have no need of magistrates, just a sharp knife.'

Master Ariston shuddered at the thought and stuck his purse back under his belt. 'I must say, the gods have blessed you with a rare talent, Thrax. You pick up on the tiniest details. I have a good mind to report the barber and his finger-chopping friends to the archon but I don't want to spoil tonight for the sake of a few coins. And I do want to visit his establishment again soon. I hope the fool sees the error of his ways or he might only have two fingers left by then. You can't give a gentleman a good haircut with only two fingers, surely.'

'Master,' said Thrax, now that he seemed to have Master Ariston's full attention. 'I've been thinking about the oracle's prediction and...'

Ha, I thought, so that's what's been on his mind.

'The message was very clear, wasn't it,' said Master Ariston. 'No doubt about it. I am going to be a tremendous success, a shining light in the world of theatre. Now put away the mirror and fetch me my boots – no, my new sandals with the golden buckles. They're more comfortable. I hope you've oiled the leather to make it shiny. This is the most important night of my entire life. Think of it, boys! If one of those wealthy gentlemen in the audience likes my play, they will pay to have it put on at the great festival in Athens. My name will be celebrated all around the world. If I win first prize, they might even put up a statue of me in the agora. What joy! My own father would have to walk past it and nod at it every day.'

Master Ariston did a slow twirl to inspect his new chiton. He'd had it made especially for tonight and it was embroidered with a beautiful blue pattern round the edges.

Satisfied with his appearance, he put on his sandals. I handed him his new alabastron, a special one shaped like a pomegranate for good luck. He sniffed its contents before sprinkling some perfume on his face.

Thrax had been given a new chiton with a blue pattern that matched Master Ariston's. But I, who had to buy my own clothes out of my measly pay, was forced to make do with an old one. It had a few rips which my mother had carefully mended the last time I went to visit her. You could only see them if you knew where to look but I felt rather shabby as we crossed the yard towards the andron.

By now the house was buzzing with guests who had come to see the play. A few of them I recognised from the last time we had been in Corinth, but most were strangers. Still, I knew they were all powerful people who could make or break Master Ariston's new career. Master Zenon bustled in with an older man by his side. This gentleman was dressed in a purple himation that reached his feet, and he kept wiping his sweaty forehead with a piece of white cloth.

'This is my friend Dymas,' Master Zenon said to Master Ariston. 'He knows your father as well. We were all in the navy together.'

Dymas insisted on sitting on a couch at the back of the room, where he could observe the audience's reaction to the play. He was soon joined by a familiar face whose voice boomed across the andron.

'Thrax! Nico! How are you, boys?'

It was Odius the Elder, a famous magistrate whom we had befriended the year before. He had been an important figure in our adventure, and had saved our lives.

'They're well, thanks,' answered Master Ariston on our behalf. 'A bit nervous like me. A lot is riding on tonight's performance.'

'I'm sure it'll all be fine,' said the archon as he settled back on a cushion with a loud, contented sigh.

Master Zenon nodded at Ahmose, his Egyptian chief-of-staff, and slaves appeared as if out of nowhere bearing dishes of food and jugs full of wine. Earlier in the afternoon I'd been hungry. I'd even tried sneaking into the kitchen in the hope that Cook would give me one of her delicious honey cakes. But suddenly I was too nervous to eat.

Master Ariston was right. A lot was riding on tonight's performance. What if the audience really did like the play – enough for someone to stage it in Athens? That would mean Master Ariston's dream would have come true. But it would also mean he would be a travelling poet no longer. We would stay at home in Athens. There would be no more travelling, and perhaps no more mysteries to solve...

'I know what you're thinking,' Thrax whispered into my ear as we sat on the floor near Master Ariston's couch.

'Do you?' I said, surprised.

He smiled. 'You look troubled but you needn't be, take my word for it. I've analysed the...'

His words were cut short by Ahmose, who clapped loudly. 'Gentlemen, we thank the gods and Master Zenon for their generosity in providing us with food and wine tonight. The performance is about to start but please keep your cups. And just nod at one of the household staff if you need more wine.'

As the slaves cleared away the dirty dishes, I noticed Ahmose drawing a silk curtain across the back door of the andron.

I nudged Thrax. 'Look.'

Two figures appeared behind the curtain. They both sat down, one on a throne-like chair with a tall back, the second one on a stool. I knew who they were right away. Our friend Fotini and Gaia, her slave girl. Women are not usually allowed to sit with men in the andron but I guess some girls are too powerful and clever to be held back by silly rules.

Just then Master Zenon showed in a late guest. A murmur ran through the audience as he took a seat right at the front of the andron.

'It's Euripides,' Master Ariston squealed at Odius. 'Why, the dear fellow has come to see my debut. I am so honoured.'

'I believe he is in town rehearsing a new play,' said Odius. 'Master Zenon invited him to come and listen to the reading.'

Slaves moved the lamps to one end of the andron where a small platform had been set up as a stage. Their light fell on a statue of Dionysus, the god of theatre, which Master Zenon had bought especially for tonight. A musician came in and played the harp. He was a short fellow with wide shoulders and he wore a grinning mask with closed eyes. I had never seen one like it before and wondered how he could play the harp so well without seeing. When he finished, four actors in masks and flowing himations appeared onstage. They carried scrolls in their hands, to read the various parts out loud. One of them announced the name of the play – *The Dolphins* by Ariston of Athens.

Master Ariston had based his play on a legend about the god Apollo travelling to take over the oracle at Delphi in the shape of a dolphin. It's a sacred story, well known by all, but he had turned it into a comedy, with dolphins singing

rude songs and Apollo smashing his lyre on a water nymph's head.

The audience were confused by the jokes at first. There were a few titters, but mostly embarrassed silence. The actors, feeling the tension, started fluffing their lines.

Gradually, as the performance continued, the silence turned to raucous laughter. It lasted till the final line of the play when the actors stood up and took off their masks. The audience rose to its feet, cheering and shouting.

'Well,' roared a sea captain who I'd seen at a symposium before. 'Those actors were brave men indeed.'

'Brave?' questioned Master Ariston.

'It takes courage to stand in front of an audience and perform rubbish like that.'

Master Ariston's face turned a bright scarlet. 'Did you not hear the merriment, sir? The audience loved my work. They laughed at every one of my clever jokes. Perhaps you don't understand satire. How about we ask the great Euripides for his opinion?'

He turned to the front of the andron, but the famous playwright had already slipped away.

'My dear fellow,' sneered the sea captain. 'The audience wasn't laughing at your jokes. It was laughing at YOU. You've got some nerve coming to Corinth looking for sponsorship. Your work is terrible, absolutely without merit. You're no more a playwright than I am a dancing river nymph.'

CHAPTER 2

A Ship in the Night

'Poor Master Ariston is devastated,' I said. 'His career as a playwright is finished before it even started.'

Thrax and I were sitting with Fotini and Gaia in their quarters, eating the last of the summer figs and grapes. The house was deathly quiet after the hubbub of the play. The windows were open to let in the night breeze. We had to speak quietly because men are strictly forbidden from visiting the women's part of the house, the gynaikon.

41

'I did try to warn him that he might not have interpreted the oracle's advice correctly,' replied Thrax. 'The more I thought about it, the more I realised the Pythia meant that people would laugh at *him*, rather than the jokes in his comedy. Sadly, I was right.'

'I should imagine your master will go back to singing and poetry,' said Fotini, 'and you two will continue to visit interesting places. I wish Gaia and I would come with you, and I dare say we will before too long.'

Master Ariston remained locked in his room for three whole days, too upset to eat or wash. Not even Thrax was allowed in to empty the chamber pot and air the room. Listening secretly at the door, we heard him cursing and tearing up papyrus scrolls.

'I shall never write another word again,' he screamed, smashing something against the wall. We guessed it was the beloved statue of Apollo that he carried with him everywhere he went.

Then on the fourth day, Cook came into the kitchen bursting with excitement. 'Master Ariston is out of his room,' she whispered grandly. 'He has come downstairs to the andron. Something very important is happening. Come with me, quick. But don't make any noise.'

Thrax and I had offered to knead the dough for the bread and were covered in flour but we tiptoed after her to the door of the andron. A small gaggle of household slaves had already gathered, eavesdropping through the curtain.

'I am sorry about what happened earlier this week, young Ariston,' we heard Master Zenon say. 'As an old friend of your father's, I feel duty-bound to help you, and my old friend Dymas here has a practical suggestion.'

Master Ariston sniffed dramatically. 'I dare not show my face outside this house, gentlemen. All of Corinth is laughing at me. And I dare not return shamefaced to Athens either. I am sure the news has travelled there by now.'

'My nephew Inacus lives on the island of Aegina,' continued Dymas in a gentle voice. 'He has asked me to find a tutor for his young son, Hero. Why don't I recommend you for the post? The men of

Corinth didn't take to your play but Zenon assures me that you are a first-class poet and singer. I'm sure my cousin will accept you as his son's teacher.'

'It will give you the opportunity to earn a decent wage until your muse returns,' said Master Zenon. 'And then you can go home with your head held high.'

Master Ariston cleared his throat. 'This is most generous of you, gentlemen. Thank you. I would like that very much.'

'Your father saved my life during a sea battle,' declared Dymas. 'I am forever in your family's debt.'

'That's settled, then,' said Master Zenon. 'Dymas will write you a letter of introduction and you can leave for Aegina as soon as you feel able to.'

The men got to their feet and the household slaves scattered before they were caught eavesdropping. Thrax managed to hide behind a potted tree but I didn't move quickly enough.

'Nico, what in the name of the gods are you doing here?' asked Master Ariston, coming through the curtain. 'You're covered in flour.'

'I… I was coming to see if you needed me to write anything down,' I murmured.

'I don't know whether I'll ever be able to write anything again,' replied Master Ariston, still feeling sorry for himself. 'The oracle's cruel joke on me has shattered my confidence. I should let you go. The sight of a stylus or a writing tablet brings me to tears. But I know you have an aged mother and father to support so I suppose I shall have to keep you on, as long as you never mention the theatre to me again. Find Thrax and give him the news. We are going to Aegina.'

Master Ariston's statue of Apollo had been smashed to bits. I helped Thrax scoop up the pieces into a bag. We couldn't throw them on the rubbish heap for fear of angering the god.

'Whatever are we going to do with them?' I wondered.

'Just put them in my trunk,' replied Thrax. 'I might be able to put the statue together again.'

It seemed an impossible task but Thrax never gives up on anything. He actually relishes doing things other people find difficult.

We aired the room, then sneaked upstairs to see Fotini and Gaia again. To our surprise, they already knew about our journey to Aegina.

'The gynaikon is directly above the andron,' Gaia explained with a giggle. 'Mistress Fotini has made a cone out of stiff linen. When we place it on the floor and put our ear to it, we can make out every word being said below.'

'And we have made our own plans too,' Fotini announced. 'Gaia and I are coming to Aegina with you.'

Thrax and I looked at her in surprise. Usually rich girls can only leave the house for festivals and trips to the temple.

'How will you manage that?' asked Thrax.

Fotini grinned. 'You know I am training to be a priestess. I shall tell my teacher at the temple of Aphrodite that I want to study and train with the priestesses of Aphaia. There is only one temple to that goddess and it's on Aegina. Father would never dare say no to a high-ranking priestess.'

'I shall bring my Medusa League pendant with me,' said Gaia. 'Just in case we have a mystery to solve when we're there.'

'You should always wear your Medusa pendant,' I replied. 'We all do. It's not only a sign that you belong to the league, the gorgon will also ward off evil and bring you good luck.'

It took three days for Dymas to write Master Ariston a letter of introduction and have it delivered to Master Zenon's house. Master Ariston kept us busy while we waited. Thrax washed and packed master's clothes. He scrubbed and polished all twenty-two items of his footwear. I helped him roll up all the scrolls in master's portable library and stow them in their wicker basket. Thrax insisted on packing them in alphabetical order, so he could find each title quickly when Master Ariston asked for it.

I mixed fresh ink to take with us, despite Master Ariston having sworn he would never write another word. I was praying to the gods he would change his mind soon. Even though his songs were as worthless as his plays, I had to admit I missed writing them down for him.

Thrax started putting the smashed statue of Apollo back together, using a powerful and invisible glue that I cooked up from the bones of animals.

By the time he'd reassembled the head and neck, the letter was delivered and it was time to leave. Ahmose helped Master Ariston clamber on to Ariana, our donkey, and Thrax handed him his precious lyre in its cedar-wood box. I made sure I had all my writing implements in my bag.

We were praying to Hermes for a safe journey when two more donkeys came trotting round the corner. Sitting on the first one were Fotini and Gaia, both wearing petasos and flowing himations. A tall man with scars on his arms led the other donkey. His name was Hector and he was a slave at the temple of Aphrodite. He would protect the girls till they returned home. A priestess from the temple of Aphrodite sat on the donkey, holding an Egyptian sun umbrella over her head.

'Her name is Agathe,' Fotini informed us. 'She is my teacher.'

Master Zenon came to the front door as the donkeys started their way down the street. 'The gods go with you, my daughter.'

Fotini waved back. Her mother had come to the doorway too, her face hidden behind a shawl.

'Goodbye, Father, Mother! Please don't worry. Great Aphrodite will protect me and Gaia.'

Corinth lies on the western side of a stretch of land known as the Isthmus of Corinth. At the other end, on the eastern side, is a busy port called Cenchrea. From here we would take a ship to the island of Aegina.

We travelled along a well-known road called the Diolkos. It is as busy as it is famous. Sailors drag their ships along it. It saves them having to sail all the way round the southern part of the mainland, where the sea is often stormy and pirates are a constant danger. Thrax and I had made the journey before so we knew what sights to point out to the girls.

As luck would have it, when we reached Cenchrea, we found a merchant ship ready to sail. It was heading for Egypt but it would stop at Aegina on the way, to deliver grain and pick up olives. With the donkeys safely stowed at the stern, we offered sacrifice to Poseidon for a safe journey.

'I hope the great god hasn't found out about Master Ariston smashing that statue,' said Fotini. 'He might put a curse on this ship.'

Gaia's eyes grew wide with horror. 'But the gods know EVERYTHING.'

We offered a generous helping of barley seeds to make sure Poseidon would not stay angry with Master Ariston. The ship shuddered as the oarsmen manoeuvred it out of the harbour and the captain ordered the sail to be raised.

The sea around Aegina and its sister islands is always busy with ships of every kind. In the fading light, we saw merchant traders like ours, almost capsizing under the weight of their cargo. We spotted triremes with their banks of oars rising and falling, and little fishing boats setting out with hunting nets for squid and octopus.

But as night fell, the sea was deserted, as captains were fearful of pirates and treacherous rocks. Our ship should have stayed in harbour till dawn but a rich passenger had paid the captain to sail through the night. His elderly father was dying and he wanted him to sign important documents before Hades claimed his spirit.

Thrax, Fotini, Gaia and I were picking out the constellations when someone behind us gasped. A black trireme was bearing down on us at great speed. The crew panicked when they saw it and many of them kissed their thumb to ward off danger.

'Children, keep your heads below the bulwarks and hold on tight,' ordered the captain. 'She might slam into us.'

As we squatted in the dark, I could hear the trireme's piper on his aulos.

Toot... toot... toot...

Every burst on that musical instrument brought the black vessel dangerously closer to ours. Now we could see its sail clearly. It had an enormous golden mask painted on it. Two figures stood at the prow, their faces gleaming in the pale moonlight. Both were shrouded with himations and wore masks. The one on the taller man matched the giant image on the sail but I couldn't see the second one clearly.

Behind the men stood a group of hoplites. They too had masks on, shiny black ones that seemed to glow in the moonlight and made them look like myrmidons – the savage human ants of legend.

The trireme rushed closer and closer towards us and we thought we were going to be skewered.

'You were right, mistress,' screamed Gaia, clinging to Fotini. 'Poseidon has put a curse on us.'

I was about to agree but at the last moment the trireme swerved and sailed in a tight curve around the hull. Our poor little ship bobbed helplessly in its wake, like a fig leaf in an overflowing gutter.

The last thing I saw, before the night swallowed the black ship, was one of the two shrouded figures. It had come to the stern and was doing a wild dance, waving its arms above its head.

Its voice carried on the wind. 'We scared you, ha ha ha…'

Its mask, I noticed, was made of silver and it leered at us with the hideous face of a drunken Dionysus.

CHAPTER 3

A Party in Aegina

'Well,' said Hector when our ship had stopped bobbing. 'Everyone's heard rumours of the pirate with the golden mask but I never thought I would actually see him with my own eyes. He really does exist.'

'I heard he comes and goes as he pleases,' added the ship's captain, 'with no regard for any law. The Athenian army has been after him for years but with no success. He keeps attacking ships and plundering coastal towns without mercy.'

'And it seems he has a sidekick,' said Master Ariston. 'A young pirate in a silver mask. I saw it leering at me with a hideous grin. I'm going to have nightmares for the rest of my life.'

'The pirate in the silver mask is new to me,' admitted the captain. 'But the danger seems to be over now. They must have bigger plunder in their sights tonight. Let's stop for a moment to thank Poseidon for his protection and then we'll continue on our way.'

Our prayer said, the rowers set to with renewed strength and by morning we reached Aegina. The island has two harbours; one for commercial ships like ours, and another used by its navy, which was only second to that of Athens in its power. We docked at the first harbour, itching to get back on to dry land.

I had heard a lot about Aegina. It is one of the richest islands in the world, famous for its sculptors, potters and jewellery makers. Its citizens are often at loggerheads with the people of Athens but they always make them welcome. I also knew that our old enemy from Delphi,

Abantes the corrupt priest, had lived here before he worked in the famous oracle.

Hector and Sister Agathe whisked Fotini and Gaia off before we had time to make plans, or even say a proper goodbye. Sister Agathe did not think it was fitting for a rich girl to be seen on the docks like a common slave.

'We'll meet soon,' called Fotini as the donkey started on its way. 'I'll send you a message as soon we are settled at the temple. I know where you are: Inacus the merchant's house.'

It turned out that our new host Inacus lived in the city behind the port. We passed through the city walls, which had many gates and towers overlooking the sea, and someone directed us to his house. A burly slave answered our knocking, snatched the letter of introduction out of Master Ariston's hand and promptly slammed the door in our face.

It opened again only a few moments later and we were let into a shady courtyard roofed over with grapevines. A short man in an expensive linen chiton came out of an andron to meet us. He had straight black hair cut in a fringe across his forehead. I guessed he was in his late thirties but his face was already lined, showing he spent a lot of time out in the sun, perhaps while travelling.

'I do apologise for keeping you outside in the heat,' he said to Master Ariston. 'My slave, Jason, mistook you for a craftsman looking for payment. I am Inacus the rope merchant.'

'Think nothing of it,' sniffed Master Ariston. 'We have travelled all the way from Corinth without stopping. I trust I look less than my usual immaculate self. I am Ariston of Athens.'

The burly slave appeared behind his master to usher us into a small but beautifully decorated andron. The walls were covered in brightly coloured mosaics of ships and sea monsters. The ships were laden with huge coils of shiny rope. Gods in gold-embellished chitons were hovering in the sky, keeping the monsters away from the ships.

Inacus sat down to read Dymas's letter again while Master Ariston perched on the edge of a second couch. 'This is most impressive,' the

merchant said after a while. 'You have achieved a lot in your long and eventful life, sir. Performing at symposiums and weddings for so many well-connected people. I shall be glad to hire you as a tutor for my son and I shall pay you—' He bent down to whisper the amount in Master Ariston's ear.

'I say,' exclaimed our master. 'That is very generous indeed.'

'My son Hero has no head for commerce,' said Inacus, 'so I should be glad if you could turn him into a poet like yourself.'

'It will be a pleasure, sir,' our master beamed. 'I shall do my very best.'

Hero is away today, visiting relatives,' said Inacus. 'You can use the time to settle in before you start lessons tomorrow. I have given you the most comfortable guest room in the house. And of course your boys are welcome to share my slaves' quarters.'

He turned and smiled at Thrax and myself. 'My own slaves say life here is pleasant. Merchants in Aegina can be very heavy-handed with their staff but I am not one of them. I do not approve of flogging, nor starving people to death. And Cook runs a generous kitchen for everyone under my roof.'

'Nico, the chubby one, is not a slave,' Master Ariston pointed out. 'He is my scribe. But he'll not object to sharing the slaves' quarters. It's where he sleeps at home.'

Inacus got to his feet, indicating that our audience with him was over. 'That's all settled, then. Welcome to my house. I'll ask Jason here to take you to your quarters and show you where to stable the donkey.'

He was about to step out of the andron, when he stopped and turned. 'I say,' he said to Master Ariston. 'I've been invited to a symposium tonight. I don't suppose you'd like to come with me? Most of the guests will be dull merchants who'll talk about trade and taxes all night. It would be fun to have an artist in our midst.'

'I'm afraid I am not performing at the moment,' replied Master Ariston. 'I haven't been very well.'

'I didn't mean you should come as the entertainment,' said Inacus. 'I want you to be my personal guest. It would be a great opportunity for you to start meeting the good and great of Aegina.' He winked at Thrax and myself. 'And I want everyone to know my son has a real live tutor from Athens. The best money can buy.'

Master Ariston puffed up his chest at Inacus's flattery. 'Then I shall be honoured to attend, sir. And I'll bring the boys with me. It'll show the other guests that your son's tutor can afford a personal slave and a scribe.' He turned to us. 'Hurry up, Thrax. You need to unpack my best clothes and air them ready for tonight.'

The symposium was held in a magnificent house at the other end of the city. As Inacus – or Master Inacus as Thrax and I had to call him now – had predicted, the guests were mostly merchants. Most of them arrived on horseback, a couple in chariots. Now they reclined on couches, enjoying the food, the wine, and a performance by jugglers and acrobats. Thrax stood behind Master Ariston's couch, ready to refill his kylix. There was nothing for me to do, so I stood beside Thrax, watching the audience and imagining they were listening to one of my adventure stories. And that's how I spotted a familiar face entering the room.

It was Gorgias, the merchant from New Sybaris. He'd been in Delphi at the same time as us, to consult the oracle about a stolen ring. A broad grin appeared on his face the moment he saw me, and he made a beeline for our couch.

'Why, Nico. Thrax. Master Ariston. What are you doing in Aegina? I thought you were in Corinth, putting on a play.'

'The oracle was mistaken about my success,' spluttered Master Ariston, making space on his couch for Gorgias and indicating for Thrax to plump up the cushions. 'My play was a complete disaster. I guess the people of Corinth are not ready for my kind of satire.'

'I am fast losing faith in oracles myself,' declared Gorgias, accepting a cup of wine. 'The Pythia said my lost ring would be found by a scribe and a slave, which I took to be your Nico and Thrax. But she was wrong. The ring has been found by someone else. I have just arrived in Aegina to collect it.'

CHAPTER 4

The Ring of the Harpies Again

Here I should tell you a little about Gorgias and our adventure in Delphi. The ring he was talking about is a priceless treasure, a golden band decorated with two harpies. Gorgias's brother Kosmas had entrusted it to him moments before he died. Gorgias was to pass it on to Kosmas's daughter, a girl Gorgias had never met. But before he could find the girl, the ring disappeared. Someone stole it.

Thrax and I had worked out that the thief was Milo, Gorgias's son, who'd used it to pay off some of his gambling debts. But by then its whereabouts were unknown. The gang of criminals Milo gave it to had disappeared with it.

The oracle predicted Thrax and I would recover the ring. And Gorgias had offered us money if we could find it. His brother had said a curse would fall on him if he didn't pass the ring on to the girl. But this time it seemed that the oracle really was wrong. Our investigations had led nowhere. Meanwhile, Gorgias had kept on looking for the ring himself. And now he'd found it.

'How *did* you manage that?' asked Master Ariston.

'I have friends in many city-states and islands,' replied Gorgias. 'One of them is a sculptor called Onatas, who lives in Aegina. I sell a lot of his work back home. He met a collector of antique jewellery who had seen it.

'This man, a retired merchant, was offered the ring by a crooked dealer. I guess the gang who took it off Milo were trying to sell it on. They must have accomplices in every city-state and island of Hellas, and probably beyond. When I got word about it from Onatas, I instructed him to buy it on my behalf. As you can imagine, it cost me an arm and a leg but I am thrilled to be able to keep my promise to my dead brother, and to evade the curse associated with the ring.'

'Imagine being cursed by harpies!' Master Ariston sniffed grandly. 'They'd poop on your food every time you tried to eat. You'd never be invited to a symposium again.'

'Quite,' said Gorgias. He looked from Master Ariston to Thrax and myself. 'I am collecting the ring from Onatas first thing tomorrow morning. Why don't you join me? I'm sure you'd like to see the wonderful treasure at last.'

CHAPTER 5

A Nasty Surprise

Onatas's home was a sprawling farm on a hill behind the city. Inacus had sent word that we were visiting and he came out to meet us as Thrax and I trudged up the path behind Gorgias in his chariot. The sculptor had a wide chest and huge muscly arms, which I reckon he got from chipping away at marble all day long.

'Our host looks terrible,' whispered Master Ariston, who was bringing up the rear on Ariana. 'I don't mean his physique. I mean his pallor. He looks like a shade from the underworld.'

'And he's walking rather slowly,' I said, 'as if he had too much wine yesterday.'

Onatas did indeed look bleary-eyed and his skin was ashen. 'I do apologise for my appearance,' he said, shaking our hands. 'I ate something bad yesterday. I keep throwing up and my head swims if I try to move too fast. But my slave Smilis is looking after me, aren't you, Smilis?'

Smilis was a boy of about seven or eight. The stubble on his head was fair, almost gold, and he had unusually green eyes. His arms were so thin they looked like sticks. An amulet to ward off the evil eye dangled from a leather thong at his throat. He stood shyly behind Onatas, shivering in the morning cold. I felt sorry for him right away.

'Take the gentleman's donkey to the stable and give her some straw, Smilis,' said Onatas. 'Then ask Cook to make me another of her healing potions.'

Smilis stepped up to Gorgias's chariot.

'Not the horse, the donkey.' Onatas smiled patiently and turned to us. 'I've had the boy since he was little. Poor thing, he's not very bright but he's faithful as a puppy. I believe his parents were Spartan and left him out to die when he was a baby. No one wants a weakling for a son.'

Onatas showed us into a small andron furnished with just two couches and a few small side tables. The walls were a rough brick, painted brilliant white to act as a backdrop to the many sculptures in the room. His house, Onatas explained, used to be a farm. He had added a bathroom and the andron.

Master Ariston threw himself down on one of the couches, marvelling at how soft it was, but Gorgias remained standing.

'It's great to see you again, old friend,' said Onatas. 'You look well. I suppose you are eager to get your hands on the ring?'

'I'll offer sacrifice to Athena when it's in my possession again,' replied Gorgias. 'You have done me proud, Onatas.'

'I did have to haggle for it,' said the sculptor. 'The crooked dealers kept increasing the price the moment they sniffed money. But I managed to secure it for you.'

'You must tell me how much I owe you. And that includes payment for your time. I know you are a very busy man.'

Onatas rubbed his ailing tummy. 'You have been a patron of mine for many years, Gorgias. It has been an honour to help. Come on, let's fetch that ring. It's in my workshop.'

We left the farmhouse and crossed an overgrown meadow towards a hulking whitewashed building that had once been a barn. Onatas unlocked a huge double door with a key from a metal ring on his belt, and we all filed in.

I was expecting the place to be dark because there were no windows, but light streamed in through a grate in the ceiling. It illuminated a crowd of bronze and marble statues. A few were of gods, which I recognised by the symbols in their hands. Athena had an owl. Zeus was hurling a thunderbolt. Demeter carried a bunch of ripe corn. Most of the others were athletes wearing laurel wreaths. There was even a half-finished charioteer in a long chiton.

Onatas marched up to a wooden chest on his workbench. 'The ring is in here, gentlemen.'

We gathered round while he selected a second key from the metal ring. It turned smoothly in the lock without making a sound. Onatas threw back the lid to reveal a collection of tools: chisels, a mallet and a small axe. He removed them one by one till the chest was empty.

We looked up from it, puzzled.

'Where's the ring?' asked Master Ariston.

'Behold, gentlemen,' said the sculptor, tapping the side of his nose to show us he was being crafty. He pressed on the bottom of the chest with both thumbs and it flipped up, revealing a secret compartment.

I caught a glimpse of a leather purse, a few silver amulets on chains and a tiny woollen packet, bound up with a knotted leather thong. Onatas picked it up carefully and handed it to Gorgias.

'Here is your ring, sir.'

Gorgias stared at the packet for a moment, his hand trembling.

'Allow me,' said Onatas. He took the packet and carefully loosened the thong. Something shone on his palm as he peeled away the woollen cloth. But it wasn't the golden ring of the harpies. It was just a polished stone marble, the kind young children play with on the street.

The ring of the harpies was nowhere to be seen.

CHAPTER 6

A New Case for the Medusa League

'It's been stolen,' gasped Master Ariston.

Gorgias stared at the marble in horror, his jowls quivering.

'But no one could have got into my tool chest,' protested Onatas. 'It was securely locked, and so was the door to the workshop.'

'Then it must have fallen out of the parcel before you put it in the chest,' said Master Ariston. 'It must be on the floor. Come on, Thrax. Nico. Make yourself useful. Start looking for it.'

'No,' said Thrax in a loud voice. 'Everyone stay where you are. Don't move.'

Everyone turned towards him.

'The ring wasn't lost. Master Ariston was right the first time. It's been stolen. We mustn't disturb the scene of the crime. We might destroy any clues left by the thief.'

Gorgias looked up from the stone marble, which Onatas was still holding. He had the appearance of a man who had just woken from a nightmare. 'Thank the gods you are here, boy. The oracle at Delphi may be right after all. I am sorry I doubted her words but how was I to know the ring would be stolen a second time? The offer I made you in Delphi still stands. Find the ring, and I will pay you handsomely.'

'Nico and I will do everything we can to retrieve it, sir,' said Thrax. 'A very clever crime has been committed here but a thief ALWAYS leaves tell-tale clues, and they always lead to his conviction.'

He turned to Onatas. 'May we leave the workshop as quickly as possible? And can you leave the tool chest unlocked? But lock the workshop door. No one must come in till Nico and I have had a good look over it.'

'Not even Onatas himself?' exclaimed Master Ariston. 'Boys, the master sculptor has work to do.'

'It won't be a problem staying away from the workshop until the boys have examined it,' replied Onatas. 'I'm too poorly to wield a mallet right now, and I have important clients to visit in town later this afternoon.'

Back in the andron, Smilis and an older slave appeared with cups and jugs of wine. Cook came in too, with a herbal potion for Onatas's nausea. It stank to the heavens.

'No water in my wine, please,' said Gorgias, sitting on the edge of a couch. 'I need something strong to revive my spirits. I can't believe the ring has slipped through my fingers again. Every time I think I can fulfil my promise to my dead brother, something happens to thwart me.'

Smilis started filling Gorgias's cup. 'Did you not hear the master, you silly boy?' snapped

Onatas. 'He wants pure wine to calm his nerves. Go and fetch a second jug and make sure the wine is undiluted.'

'I'll see to it myself, sir,' said Cook, leading a confused Smilis away. The older slave followed them.

Thrax nodded at the tablet stuck under my belt. 'Nico, take notes.' He turned to Onatas. 'When did you obtain the ring?'

'Five days ago,' replied Onatas. 'I brought it straight home and locked it in the tool chest.'

'Master Gorgias said you were told about the ring by a jewellery collector. Does he know you bought it?'

Onatas put down his cup. 'I assume he doesn't. I don't know him very well. I only see him at social functions but he has the reputation of being a very honest man. He can't be the thief.

'The ring came up in conversation at a symposium. I was saying how I hate sculpting mythological creatures. They're so old-fashioned. The collector mentioned the ring and how beautifully carved the harpies on it were. He said they looked so life-like you'd believe they could fly off the ring. He said I'd change my mind about sculpting mythological beasts if I saw them. The mention of that elusive ring made me prick up my ears at once, of course. I knew my friend Gorgias was looking for it. What a piece of good luck, it turning up in Aegina. It seemed the gods wanted him to have it back. I asked the collector where he'd seen it and I bought it from the crooked dealer the very next morning.'

'Did you tell anyone you hid the ring in the tool chest?' asked Thrax.

Onatas shook his head. 'Absolutely no one. I was alone when I opened the secret compartment and put it inside.'

'Do you ever receive visitors in your workshop?' asked Thrax. 'Clients or benefactors?'

'No, I only see guests in the andron. I don't feel comfortable when people look at my work before it's completely finished.'

'And when was the last time you saw the ring?'

'Yesterday, late afternoon,' replied Onatas. 'I opened the tool chest to get some money from the purse. I was going to a symposium and I wanted some coins to throw at the dancers.'

'And you weren't feeling ill then?'

'No, I only started feeling ill at the symposium.'

'But did you actually see the ring when you went to get the money, or just the woollen parcel?' asked Thrax.

'I saw the ring itself,' said Onatas. 'I took it out to admire it. My friend the collector was right. The harpies were some of the best work I've ever seen. It made me think I should accept commissions to carve beasts from the ancient stories after all.'

Thrax glanced at me to make sure I was writing down everything Onatas was saying. 'And you went straight to the symposium after that?'

'That's right.'

'Who was left in the house?'

'No one,' said Onatas. 'Smilis and Timon – that's the older slave you've just seen – came with me to the symposium. Telephassa our cook went to the temple. No one else lives in the house. I am not married.'

'I imagine you were in the workshop earlier that day. Did any of the slaves come in during that time?'

Onatas nodded. 'Telephassa brought me some food. Timon helped me move a heavy statue and Smilis came to watch me work. He likes doing that, especially when I'm carving animals. Sometimes he models for me.'

'And you are absolutely sure you locked the tool chest and the door to the workshop when you left?'

'Quite sure,' replied Onatas without hesitation. 'In fact I checked twice.'

'What time was this?'

'The last hour of the day. Sunset.'

'And I assume you took the keys to the symposium with you?'

'The keyring never leaves my belt,' said Onatas. 'It is on me day and night.'

'And were Smilis and Timon with you all evening?' asked Thrax.

'Smilis was with me in the andron. The boy might be foolish but he's very caring. He looked after me all night, especially when I started feeling out of sorts. He kept sending to the kitchen for herbal drinks. I should have come home early but there were a few potential clients at the symposium I was desperate to meet.'

'And Timon?' said Thrax.

'He was in the stables, looking after the cart and donkey. The older slaves tend to gather there, to gamble the little bit of money their masters allow them to earn.'

'And did both come home with you?' asked Thrax.

'Yes,' said Onatas. 'They went straight to bed and Cook arrived from the temple some time later. She made me a potion for my stomach. We have no slave quarters on the farm. Cook and Smilis sleep by the fire in the kitchen. Timon sleeps in a small hut next to the house, to keep watch over the goats.'

'And could anyone have broken into the workshop at night, while you were sleeping?'

'I didn't go to sleep,' declared Onatas. 'I can't sleep when I'm poorly. I spent the night in the workshop, gulping down potions and working on sketches for my next work.'

'And are you sure the lock on the workshop door had not been tampered with?' Thrax asked.

'As sure as I am sitting here talking to you,' replied Onatas. 'I am very careful about these things. The statues in my workshop are worth a fortune.'

'And the house itself had not been touched? You didn't find any signs that someone had been through the andron, or your bedroom, looking for the ring?'

Onatas shook his head. 'Cook and Timon would have noticed if someone had been in the house.'

'So,' cut in Master Ariston who had been listening on the edge of his seat. 'The ring was stolen from a locked tool chest, in a locked workshop with no windows. Yet the thief managed to get in and out. How did he do it? Is he a spirit?'

'I assure you he's flesh and bone like you and me, master,' said Thrax.

Master Ariston shook his head. 'It's a baffling mystery. Good luck on solving it, boys.'

CHAPTER 7

A Secret Meeting Place

Thrax would have loved to search the workshop for clues right then but Master Ariston dragged us away. He had to give Hero his first lesson later that morning. He was so anxious about it, he forgot to give us a list of chores to do while he was teaching.

'I think we need to have a meeting,' said Thrax.

I looked around the slaves' room, which had a few rickety old couches around the walls. Tattered himations were spread out on the floor for beds. 'Let's find a proper meeting place,'

I said. 'Somewhere we won't be disturbed or overheard. This house is teeming with slaves and household staff.'

We slipped out, closing the door behind us. The houses on the street were all spacious and well kept but at one end we came across an abandoned one. Most of its walls had collapsed, leaving mounds of mud bricks and broken roof tiles in the weeds.

'Ha,' I said, 'what an interesting place. It seems to have been hit by a thunderbolt.'

'This house was knocked down by the authorities,' Thrax corrected me. 'Look, you can tell they started from the roof because the tiles are all trapped under the mud bricks, which were pulled down later.'

I stared at the devastation around me. 'Why would the authorities pull down a house?'

'It's a common enough punishment,' Thrax said. 'The people who lived here must have broken the law in a big way. Perhaps they committed murder, or insulted the gods.'

'Where are they now?' I wondered.

'Sent into exile, I should imagine,' said Thrax. 'Never to return home.'

I shuddered to think what it must feel like losing your home and being forced to live far from the people and places you loved.

'Let's explore,' I said.

The foundations of the house poked through the weeds and couch grass. A broken bread oven lay on its side in a corner of what had once been a kitchen. The faded reeds of a bread basket lay crushed underneath it. Something slithered inside it as I came closer. I caught a flash of yellow and brown scales. An adder. The oven had become home to a venomous snake. It hissed at me and I stepped back in a hurry.

Up against the remnants of one wall stood an altar with a headless statue on it. It was painted black on one side and white on the other. I shrank back from it in fear. 'This is an altar to Melinoe,' I gasped, 'the dark goddess of ghosts and a bringer of nightmares and madness. Who would have such a statue in their yard?'

'This bit of the house wasn't the yard,' Thrax said. 'It used to be the andron.'

'That's even worse. People used to gather here to offer sacrifice to the most terrible goddess in the pantheon. No wonder they brought misfortune on themselves.'

We moved away from the headless statue, further into the ruins, where we found an old well. Behind it, the lower half of a back wall was still standing, with a door hanging askew in it. There were traces of frescoes on the wall: the outline of a sea nymph holding a shell. A sunken boat full of ghostly sailors. Their round mouths were wide open in horror.

Thrax tugged at the door and it opened. We found ourselves looking into a small orchard, full of fig trees gone wild. Overripe fruit hung on the branches, attracting wasps and sparrows. Their buzzing and chittering filled the air. Behind the trees, a red-tiled roof glowed in the sunshine.

We picked our way carefully through stinging nettles to discover a small outhouse, derelict and long-forgotten. The authorities had obviously missed it when they pulled down the rest of the house, or perhaps they thought it was not worth their time demolishing it.

It had a warped door with a handle shaped like a seahorse, and a window blocked up with a bird's nest, long-abandoned. Thrax let us in.

When our eyes got used to the dark, we saw old farm tools piled in a corner. A large harvest basket hung on a wall. Below it stood a krater with only one handle, and next to it a three-legged table. Someone had left a chipped drinking cup on it. Everything was covered in a thick layer of dust and cobwebs.'

'This used to be a gardener's store and hideaway,' said Thrax.

'And now it can be our secret meeting place,' I added. 'It's perfect. We can clean it up and bring a store of snacks for when we have meetings. Come on, let's get started.'

Thrax made brooms out of twigs and I filled the krater at the well. Before long we had splashed water all over the place and swept the wet dust out into the orchard. Thrax unblocked the window. At last the hut sparkled like a newly minted coin.

A quick hunt in the weeds yielded more treasure: two wobbly stools. We gave them a good wipe and carried them inside. Now it looked like a proper meeting place. All we needed was a small lamp for night meetings and some flowers in a jar to make it smell nice.

'I think it's time we had our first meeting,' said Thrax, sitting down on one of the stools.

I took out my tablet.

'Read me the notes you have written. I want to make sure I remember every detail correctly.'

I read them out carefully and Thrax listened, his eyes focused on the sunshine outside the open door. 'Hmm,' he said when I finished. 'The ring was in the tool chest when Onatas left for the symposium at sunset but it was gone by the time he opened the parcel in front of us this morning. He was in the workshop all night, so the ring must have been stolen while he was at the symposium.'

I tapped on the table with my stylus. 'His slaves were all out of the house. It must have been a wandering robber.'

'A robber would have taken the money and the silver amulets too,' said Thrax. 'No, this thief wanted only the ring. It had to be someone who *knew* it was there.'

'But Onatas insists that he was alone when he locked the ring in the tool chest,' I pointed out, 'and he told no one about it.'

Thrax smiled. 'That could only mean one thing. Someone must have been spying on him.'

'Exactly. And we need to find out who had the opportunity.'

I scratched a plan of Onatas's farmhouse in my tablet. 'Onatas says he never receives guests at the workshop, only in the andron, which is in another building completely. I suppose one of them might have sneaked across the meadow without being noticed.'

'Guests are never left unattended in a house,' said Thrax. 'A slave stays with them all the time.'

'That only leaves the slaves themselves, then. Smilis, Timon and Telephassa.'

'They are the main suspects,' Thrax agreed. 'Write down their names.'

I smudged out the plan of Onatas's farmhouse to make space for the names. 'Smilis doesn't look like he could steal a honey cake from a griddle let alone break into a workshop without leaving a trace,' I said, 'which leaves Timon and Telephassa.'

Thrax shifted on his stool. 'We'll have to investigate all three. Never leave a stone unturned, I say.'

'Hey,' I said suddenly, adding a fourth name to the list, 'you don't think Onatas could have stolen the ring himself, do you?'

'Good thinking, Nico, but I'm afraid it wasn't him. I watched his face closely when he realised the ring had been stolen. No one could have faked the shock and look of horror in his eyes. He wasn't pretending.'

I rubbed out Onatas's name with my thumb. 'Why did the thief leave the marble in place of the ring, I wonder?'

'It might just have been a joke. Some thieves have a very peculiar sense of humour. But it might have been to give the parcel some weight. If Onatas picked it up but did not look in it, he would not have discovered the ring had been stolen.

'But let's concentrate on our three suspects. They all say that they were away from the house and the workshop. Smilis seems to have an alibi, Onatas himself. We need to check on the other two. Could one of them have sneaked back to the workshop while Onatas was lying on the couch at the symposium and stolen the ring? It's time to find out. Let's go and take a look at the workshop.'

'Good idea,' I said, 'but let's stop and get some lunch at Inacus's house on the way. Thinking always makes me hungry.'

CHAPTER 8

Footprints in the Dust

Coming out of the ruined house, we ran into Smilis. He was carrying a heavy basket on his shoulder and pulling a wooden horse on wheels behind him. The basket smelled sharp and briny and we could see fish tails sticking out of it.

'Good day, Smilis,' said Thrax.

Smilis beamed from ear to ear. 'Good day, kyrios.'

'I am no master,' replied Thrax. 'I am a slave like you. That basket looks heavy. Where are you going with it?'

'To Master Inacus's house. It's a gift from his friend Master Onatas.' Smilis let go of the wooden horse and tried moving the basket from his right shoulder to the left.

Thrax took it from him. 'I'll carry it for you,' he said. 'We're on our way there. You look after your toy horse.'

'Thank you, kyrios.'

Thrax nodded at Smilis's bare feet. 'Your feet are all wet. Did you go and play with the other children in the fountain at the agora?'

Smilis looked guilty. 'Horsey wanted a drink.'

'You should have washed your face while you were there,' laughed Thrax. 'It's all sticky. Have you been scoffing pomegranates?'

Smilis nodded and tried to wipe it clean.

'Well don't let Telephassa find out about it or you'll be in trouble. Now go home before anyone notices how long you've been away.'

We'd missed lunch by the time we got to Inacus's house but the cook gave us honey cakes, which we wolfed down out in the yard. Master Ariston's voice boomed out of the andron.

'Now, Hero, I must tell you the story of Ulysses and how he managed to get past the wicked sirens...'

We tiptoed silently across the yard, praying our master wouldn't spot us and give us chores to do. Saddling Ariana, we rode over to Onatas's farm. The sculptor was getting on to his own donkey as we arrived. He was dressed in a clean chiton, ready to go into town to see his important clients.

'Good afternoon, sir,' said Thrax. 'I hope you are feeling better.'

'Much better, thank you,' said Onatas.

'We've come to look for clues in the workshop,' said Thrax. 'Please can we have the key?'

Onatas removed the key from the ring on his belt.

'Thank you, sir,' said Thrax. 'We'll be finished by the time you come back.' We passed Timon's hut on our way to the workshop. The dwelling was not much bigger than our secret meeting place. There was a pen for the goats on one side and a small vegetable patch on the other. A wooden statue stood in the middle of it. It had a horrible misshapen face with a leering grin and was painted a bright purple. Metal earrings dangled from its enormous ears. I noticed a mallet in one of its hands.

'What in the name of the gods is that?' I asked Thrax.

'It's a device to scare away the birds. We had a lot of them on the farm outside Thebes. The figure is Hephaestus, the god of smithies and Aphrodite's husband. Farmers believe he's so ugly, he scares away the birds before they can harm the crops.'

I stared at the figure. 'How can the husband of Aphrodite, the goddess of beauty, be so ugly?'

Thrax shrugged. 'It's just a myth, Nico. A story.'

Outside the workshop, Thrax inspected the lock on the door. Then he went round the outside of the barn, looking for loose bricks or hidden entrances. Finally he clambered on to the sloping roof to check the tiles and the skylight.

'This workshop is as secure as the Medusa's lair,' he said, coming down again.

The statues in the workshop stared at us with blind eyes as we pulled open the door. 'Careful,' said Thrax. 'Don't disturb anything.'

I peered down at the thick layer of gritty dust on the floor. It crunched under my feet. 'Ha,' said Thrax. 'Here are my footprints and yours, Nico. These prints going up to the workbench and back belong to Onatas.'

'How do you know?' I asked.

'I watched everyone's feet carefully this morning, to memorise the footprints. These ones on the side belong to Master Ariston. I'd know them anywhere. And these, always a couple of steps behind them, were made by Gorgias. He wears special boots that help people with a limp walk better. Notice the right foot has made heavier prints than the left ones.'

I'd never noticed Gorgias walked with a limp but then I'm not as observant as Thrax. That's why he is so good at solving mysteries.

'And I suppose these smaller prints were made by Smilis,' I said. 'I noticed he goes barefoot all the time. The poor mite probably doesn't even own a pair of sandals.'

'Neither do Timon and the cook. Look, Nico, those deep ones going towards the charioteer must be Timon's. He's got a very heavy step, which leaves very clear prints. The wider ones going up to the workbench belong to Telephassa. She has cracked skin on her heels, and it shows in the footprints.'

'When did you notice that?'

'This morning in the andron. She left sweaty footprints all over the floor.'

He squatted and looked closely at a set of footprints I hadn't noticed before.

'And who made those?' I wondered.

'Someone with money,' replied Thrax. 'They were made by a very expensive kind of sandal boot called a cothurnus. Actors wear them on stage because they're comfortable. I believe rich hunters and horsemen use them when they're in the saddle too.'

'They're almost as big as Master Ariston's.'

'But wider,' said Thrax. He put his nose close to the ground to inspect them. 'There's something not quite right about them.'

'How do you mean?'

Thrax ignored my question, got up and dusted his hands. He started walking around the workshop. Now that we had inspected the footprints around the workbench, there was no need to preserve them. He stopped at an empty plinth in a corner and bent down to run a finger along the top.

'Flour,' he said, putting his finger to his tongue.

'What do you mean, flour?'

'I mean there are traces of flour on this plinth.'

'How odd,' I said.

'Not odd at all. In fact it makes the whole picture much clearer... much clearer indeed.'

CHAPTER 9

The Ghost at the Shrine

I lay snuggled in my himation, staring up at the ceiling in our secret meeting place. Thrax and I had decided to sleep here. Inacus had a lot of slaves and there was hardly any room for us in their quarters.

It was the middle of the night but I was too excited to go to sleep. I opened my tablet and looked at our list of suspects.

1. Smilis
2. Telephassa
3. Timon

I added a fourth.

4. The person who left the mysterious
   footprints in the workshop

One of those four had committed the crime, but which one? And what had Thrax meant when he said the picture was getting clearer? I could see nothing but a tangle of impossible clues. A ring stolen from a locked tool chest. Mysterious footprints made with expensive sandal boots. Some flour on a plinth. How were these things connected?

I wished I could ask Thrax but he was snoring softly under his himation. I closed my eyes and tried to go to sleep but Hypnos, the god of slumber, would not answer my prayers.

The night was full of strange noises. Beetles munching away at the rotten beams above. Mice scampering across the floor. Owls hooting outside. I thought of the adder in the broken oven and shuddered at the thought it might crawl into the hut.

Suddenly I became aware of yet another noise. Footsteps crunching in the weeds outside. My first thought was to hide under my himation. Then curiosity got the better of me and I tiptoed out of the hut to the door in the wall. We had left it ajar and I could see through the crack very clearly.

A dark shape was flitting between the mounds of rubble. I opened the door another crack to see better. The figure reached the edge of the house, stopped for a moment to look up and down the street and then disappeared. I looked around to see where it had come from. And that's when I spotted the statue of Melinoe glowing in the moonlight. It now had a head, with two enormous eyes that seemed to be looking directly at me. The rest of her body was covered in hissing, twisting snakes…

'See,' said Thrax. 'No head. Just a broken neck on an old statue. Same as it was when we saw it yesterday.'

I stared at the statue in disbelief. Thrax had marched me out to have a second look when I'd told him what I'd seen the next morning.

'But it did have a head last night. And it was covered in snakes. I saw something else too. A dark shape floating across the ruins. A ghost – Melinoe is their goddess, isn't she?'

'Honestly! Your writer's imagination is running away with you.' Thrax shook his head and started washing his face at the well.

He was right, of course. There is no such thing as ghosts. I had imagined everything. Or perhaps I had fallen asleep without knowing and Phantasos, the god of dreams, had sent me a nightmare.

I picked some figs for our breakfast and we ate them on our way to Inacus's house. 'I hope Master Ariston doesn't have too many chores for us today,' said Thrax. 'I want to carry on with our investigations right away.'

Sadly, Thrax's wish was not to come true. 'There you are, boys,' called Master Ariston when he saw us. 'I'd started to think you had both been carried away by harpies. Thrax, could you wash one of my spare chitons? I've got ink stains on the one I'm wearing and I do want to look spotless in the classroom. And then retune my harp. Hero has a music lesson this morning. Nico, could you make some extra ink and sharpen the styluses? And could you write me a list of all the city-states in Hellas? You'll find the information in my scrolls. On best papyrus, please, so Hero can keep it after the lesson. We're doing politics and geography this afternoon.'

Master Ariston seemed to have taken to teaching like a duck to water. Perhaps it's because he's a born performer and Hero is the perfect audience. The boy certainly seemed to be enjoying his lessons, with ink stains all over his own chiton to prove it.

By the time we had finished our chores, the sun was halfway across the sky and the cicadas were singing loudly in the trees behind the house.

I met up with Thrax in the yard. 'What shall we do next?'

'First thing,' he said, 'we need to make sure that our suspects really were at the places they claim they were when the crime took place. Smilis and Timon at the symposium, Telephassa at a temple in town.'

We rode over to the farm on Ariana and talked to Onatas first. Yes, he assured us once again, Smilis had been with him at the symposium all evening. No, the slave hadn't left the side of the couch for one single moment. Onatas would have noticed if he had, because he kept cooling his face with a rhipis.

Next we interviewed Telephassa. She was scouring a blackened chytra in the kitchen. 'I was at the sanctuary of Hekate to offer sacrifice,' she explained. 'As you know, once the ritual starts, the doors to the temple are shut and no one is allowed to leave until it's finished and the meat from the sacrifice is eaten. I couldn't have got out even if I'd wanted to. I didn't get home till Master Onatas was in the workshop.'

Last of all we went to see Timon in the goat hut. He was sitting outside in the sun, skinning an eel. An old dog lay at his feet, his eyes fixed on the fish. Timon grinned when he saw us.

'Welcome, boys! Say hello, Omega. She's an old dog but a happy one.' He held up the eel for us to admire. 'By the gods, I caught a big one this morning, a giant. It's Master Onatas's favourite. Look at the meat on this thing. There's enough for all of us. We'll dine like the kings of old tonight.'

'Ha, you must be a very good fisherman to land such a big eel,' said Thrax.

'I've been fishing all my life,' grinned Timon, leaving a trail of blood across his chin as he wiped it. 'I love the peace and quiet of holding a fishing line, waiting for something to take the bait. It gives you time to sort out your thoughts, to appreciate the gods' blessings in your life. I take Smilis with me sometimes but he hasn't the patience for it. I'm afraid that boy will never be a fisherman.'

Timon turned out to have a rock-solid witness too, a friend called Priam who'd played dice with him at the stables all night. Timon told us where we could find him in the agora if we wanted to make absolutely sure he was telling the truth. Priam's master allowed him to run a fruit stall there.

I was inclined to believe Timon. He seemed a decent fellow to me, not one for stealing priceless rings. But Thrax insisted we had to make sure all our suspects' witnesses stood up to questioning. So next we went to the agora to find Priam.

'I assure you he didn't leave the gambling table for a moment,' Priam said cheerily from behind a counter piled high with ripe grapes and pomegranates. 'The old rascal was on a winning streak and I believe he went home with his purse full to bursting.'

We went to the sanctuary of Hekate after that, where the priestess confirmed that she had seen Telephassa at the temple, and that she couldn't have left till the doors were opened at the end of the long ritual.

'That rules out Onatas's three slaves,' I said on our way back to Inacus's house. 'Every one of them has a reliable witness. That leaves only the man who left the mysterious footprints. But who is he?'

CHAPTER 10

The Pond

'Ha!' Thrax stopped in the middle of the street. We had just passed the ruined house and I was wondering if I should pick a few figs from outside our meeting place. It was late in the afternoon and I was hungry.

'What's the matter, Thrax?'

He looked up and down the street. 'Come with me, Nico.'

Thrax made straight for a narrow gap, an alleyway, between two enormous houses with shuttered windows. At the far end we could see a section of the city wall, its sun-dried bricks covered in fresh lime cement. A guard was sitting at an open doorway – one of Aegina's city gates.

'Good afternoon, boys.'

'Good afternoon, sir,' we both said.

'You going out of the city?' asked the guard. He could only have been a year or two older than Thrax and wore a spotless chiton. He smelled strongly of perfume.

'Yes, sir.'

'I lock the gate at sunset,' said the guard. 'Make sure you're back by then or you'll have to walk all around the city to the main gate, which stays open longer.'

'We won't be long,' Thrax said. 'We're just looking for a good spot for fishing.'

'Ah, there's a pond not far from here where you might hook a carp or catfish. An eel too, if you're lucky. The slaves on this side of town fish there a lot. I often see them coming back with their catch. Some are even generous enough to slip me a catfish or two for Ma's cooking pot.

But you won't find anyone there in the afternoon. It's too hot for fishing.'

'We're only going to have a look,' said Thrax. 'How do we find it?'

'Just follow the path down the hill. You'll pass an old goat farm on your right. Further on you'll see an ancient olive tree with a hollow trunk. It has a small altar dedicated to Demeter inside it. Turn right there, keep on walking and you'll see the pond below you.'

We smelled the goat farm before we saw it. Two guard dogs barked ferociously as we passed the gate and bared their teeth through the bars. After a while we came to the hollow oak tree with the altar to Demeter. It stank with rotten fish left as offerings. There were pomegranates on the altar too, fruit sacred to the goddess.

At the end of the path, we saw the pond stretched out below us, a near-perfect oval of deep blue reflecting the sky. The water was smooth as Master Ariston's mirror. It was ringed with huge flat stones, which shone bone-white in the sunshine. There was no one about, just as the guard had predicted.

'Why are we here, Thrax?' I asked as we scrambled down towards it.

He didn't reply and I followed him to the edge of the water where he dipped his hand in, swirled it round a couple of times, then pulled it out and examined it carefully.

'Ha,' was all he said before he started to circle the pond, staring closely at the water. After a while, he took off his sandals and chiton and handed them to me.

'What is it?' I asked. 'What are you looking for?'

Thrax waded into the water till it came up to his chest. Then he took a deep breath to fill his lungs and dived in. When he surfaced he was clutching a large wet bag. He dragged it ashore.

'Your stylus sharpener, please, Nico.'

I handed him the knife and he slashed the bag open. A large stone fell out as he turned it upside down. It was followed by a pair of sodden sandal-boots. Cothurni. The kind that had left the unexplained footprints in Onatas's workshop.

Thrax picked one up, shook the water out of it and examined the sole carefully. 'Just as I thought. Look at this, Nico.'

I peered closely at the sandal-boot. There was something sharp stuck in it. Thrax pulled it out with his fingernails and held it in the palm of his hand.

It was a tiny fragment of marble.

'This must have come from Onatas's workshop,' I gasped. 'These sandals are the ones the thief was wearing when he stole the ring.'

'You're right, Nico. Put it carefully in your bag. We'll take the sandals too. We'll hide them in our meeting place in case we need to show them as evidence.'

I wrapped the sliver of marble in a spare piece of papyrus and stowed it carefully in my bag. 'But how did you know the cothurni were going to be in the pond? Was it one of your famous hunches?'

'No, it was just something I noticed yesterday when we met Smilis, and something Timon said earlier today. Those sandal boots are the first in a list of three clues we need to nail the thief.'

'What are the other two?'

'Make a list in your tablet, Nico. You can cross out each clue as we find it.'

I started writing.

CLUES TO SOLVE THE MYSTERY
1. SANDAL BOOTS

I put a line across that right away. We'd already found them. 'What next?'

'Clue number two,' said Thrax, 'is MARBLES. The third is KEYS.'

He put on his chiton and sandals while I wrote in my tablet. Then we trudged up the hill again.

As we passed the shrine in the olive tree, a movement on the altar caught my eye. I saw a flash of yellow and brown scales. Another adder. I leaped back, but not before I'd noticed that someone had disturbed the offerings.

One of the pomegranates was missing.

CHAPTER 11

Poison

We stopped at our meeting place to hide the sandals inside the old krater.

'Where have you been?' demanded Master Ariston when we got home, scowling fiercely to impress Hero. 'Hunting for Gorgias's ring?'

'Sort of, master,' said Thrax.

'You'll have to put the investigation aside for the moment,' said Master Ariston. 'Hero and I are composing a song about Aphaia, the goddess of Aegina, but I hardly know anything about her. No one outside this island does. I want you to go over to her temple and get some information out of your friend Fotini. Go first thing tomorrow. Inacus said one of his slaves will take you.'

I was desperate to get on with solving our new mystery but I was also delighted to be seeing Fotini and Gaia again. They'd be thrilled to hear about our latest case and Fotini, no doubt, would want to get involved.

We set out on Ariana before dawn, with a slave called Rhesus who had his own donkey. Our friend the guard was on duty at the gate again, but he was fast asleep, snoring under his himation. He still reeked of perfume.

A light mist hung in the air but the morning sun soon melted it. It was going to be another scorching day. The road to the temple, which stood at the north of the island, took us through flat land patterned with farms and well-cultivated orchards. Sometimes we rode through valleys that smelled of thyme and lavender. There were bees and large brightly coloured butterflies everywhere.

The journey was quite long, nearly three hours, and we approached our destination hot and tired. The sanctuary loomed ahead on a steep hill covered in pine trees, a small fortress of brick walls and a wide wooden gate. Thrax and I got off Ariana and finished the rest of the journey on foot. We could see a marble sphinx on a column poking up behind the wall, and the upper half of a temple with columns and a sloping, red-tiled roof.

We stopped outside the gate to admire the view. It was truly spectacular, the best I'd ever seen. Below us was a little harbour, busy with small coracles and a fish market on the quay. From where we stood, the people looked as small as ants.

Beyond the harbour, the calm sea stretched out to infinity, green close to land but a purplish blue further out.

Rhesus told us that on a clear day you could see all the way to the acropolis in Athens where the Athenians had just built a new temple to Athena.

The sanctuary of Aphaia draws women from all over the island and beyond. We stopped a temple girl and sent a message to Fotini and Gaia. They came out almost instantly, both delighted to see us.

'Hello, Thrax. Nico! What a lovely surprise. Come in. We'll show you around.'

We followed them through the wide gate, leaving Rhesus in charge of the donkeys. The sanctuary complex reminded me a little of the oracle in Delphi. There were houses for the priests and a huge altar facing a temple with columns all around it. Gaia said there were seventy-two of them.

But what took my breath away were the sculptures under the sloping roof. These showed Athena watching the Trojan War. Below her, striding across the battlefield, were the heroes Ajax and his brother Teucer.

The sun was now high up in the sky, so Fotini and Gaia took us into the priests' house for something to eat. During the meal, Fotini

explained everything she knew about Aphaia, the goddess who protected mothers at childbirth.

When I had written everything down carefully in my tablet, we told her and Gaia about our new mystery. They both listened carefully, Gaia gasping when I described the headless statue of Melinoe.

'This thief sounds very clever,' said Fotini. 'I should imagine he's an experienced professional who would stop at nothing to get away with his crime. Please be careful, boys.'

Sister Agathe, Fotini's teacher, approached our table. 'Mistress Fotini, you have a lesson soon. Please say goodbye to your friends.'

'We have to go,' said Gaia sadly. 'We have a herbal potions class.'

'You're learning to make herbal charms?' said Thrax.

Gaia smiled. 'And poisons.'

I blinked in surprise. 'You're being taught how to make poison?'

'We are learning to recognise different poisons and their effect on people,' Fotini explained. 'And how to make cures and antidotes for them.'

She pulled a small alabastron from the folds of her chiton. 'Yesterday we made a very special potion with herbs collected from the hills below the temple. It cures snakebites.' She pulled off the stopper and poured a few drops into the palm of her hand. The antidote was dark green. I thought of the adder in the ruins outside our secret meeting place. 'Can I have some, Fotini, please? I saw an adder outside our meeting place. I know the poison from adders is only strong enough to kill puppies and small children but I feel safer having the antidote.'

She handed me the alabastron. 'Yes, take it. I can make more.'

The girls showed us to the gate. 'It was very nice seeing you, boys,' said Fotini. 'I fear your lives might be in danger. Do send us a message if you need help.'

Thrax was very quiet as the temple gate shut behind us. 'Nico, take out your tablet. We need to add another clue to the list. Clue number four. POISON.'

CHAPTER 12

The Mysterious Cave

S uddenly our mystery had taken a very dark turn.

There was the warning from Fotini. And now a chilling fourth clue. Poison. How had it been used to steal the ring?' As always, Thrax wouldn't tell me when I asked.

We were riding ahead of Rhesus so he would not overhear our conversation.

'We need to search Onatas's farm,' Thrax said.

'What are we looking for?'

'Clues.'

'The poison?'

'Yes. We'll go tomorrow on foot. It's important that no one on the farm sees us or they might tamper with the evidence.'

At home, I copied Fotini's notes on best papyrus for Master Ariston. But we hurried away to the secret meeting place before he could give us any jobs for the next day. We wanted to continue with our investigation first thing in the morning.

The last of the stars had faded in the sky by the time we crested the hill and saw Onatas's farm ahead of us. The door to the workshop was already open. We could see a light burning inside and heard the clang of the sculptor's mallet.

'What do we do now?' I asked Thrax.

'We find a good hiding place from where we can observe everyone's comings and goings. When the coast is clear, we'll sneak into the farmhouse and have a good look round.'

There was an ancient carob tree close to us, with heavy brown seed pods dangling on its branches. Snuggled in its leafy branches, we had both the farmhouse and the workshop clearly in our sights. I broke off a carob pod and chewed it thoughtfully, relishing its sweet juices.

After a while Timon came out of the farmhouse, followed by Omega prancing happily around him. He let the goats out of the pen. Omega must have picked up our scent, because she came bounding over to the tree and growled fiercely.

I nearly fell off the branch in alarm.

'Come back, you silly girl,' Timon called out. 'You know you'll never be able to catch the bird in that tree. You'll just frighten her chicks to death.'

Omega barked and pawed frantically at the tree trunk before darting off. She followed Timon and the goats away from the farm. They all disappeared over the hill.

'He's taking the goats out to pasture,' said Thrax. 'He'll be gone all day.'

A few moments later, Smilis skipped out of the workshop to relieve himself in the weeds. He was wearing an oversized loincloth and had feathered wings fastened to his back. His skin was a ghostly white, as if he'd been rolling around in flour.

'He must be modelling for Onatas,' I whispered to Thrax. 'Eros, I think.'

Smilis went back inside, scratching his bottom. Nothing else happened for a while. Then the door to the farmhouse opened and Telephassa emerged with a calathus clasped to her chest. It seemed to be full of fruit. She set it down on the doorstep and looked around furtively before disappearing behind the farm. When she came back, she had a second basket dangling at her hip. Once more she took a good look around and hoisted the heavy basket on to her head.

We held our breath a second time as she passed right under our tree. 'She's on her way to the agora to sell whatever's in those baskets,' I whispered. 'The gods are smiling on us today, Thrax. She may be gone for some time too. She was acting very suspiciously though, if you ask me. I wonder what was in that smaller basket?'

The ringing of Onatas's mallet stopped abruptly. The sculptor and Smilis both came out of the workshop. Onatas sat on the grass with his back against the wall. Smilis ran over to the farmhouse and returned with a bowl of food and a heavy jug. We waited in the tree while they breakfasted on honey cakes.

The moment the coast was clear again, we slipped down from our lookout. 'Come on, Nico,' whispered Thrax, 'let's see what that cook was up to.'

We sprinted towards the farmhouse, keeping low in the tall grass. Behind it, we stopped to get our bearings. A narrow path lay in front of us, with a hen run on one side and a well-tended vineyard on the other.

We followed the path past the vineyard to a rocky patch of land. There was a brook and behind it a small cave in the rocks. The entrance was bricked up and had a door, painted bright green.

We pushed the door open. Inside, there was a curious, sickly smell coming from a lebes, a cauldron with handles, bubbling over a low fire. We slipped in to have a look around. We could make out jars and pots on a stone shelf on the wall. Huge bunches of drying herbs hung from the moss-encrusted ceiling. Below them was a stone table, scrubbed clean, with a lidded cooking pot on it.

Thrax lifted the lid. The pot was full of alabastrons just like the one Fotini had given me.

'Potions,' I said.

I didn't have time to say anything else. We heard footsteps running to the door. Someone was coming to the cave.

'Down here, Nico,' said Thrax, and we ducked under the table.

The unexpected visitor came in. I heard a grating sound as a stool was dragged across the floor to the table. There was a clink as the lid was lifted off the cooking pot and something dropped inside it.

Then the stool was dragged back in place, the feet skipped away and the door closed behind them.

Thrax and I came out from under the table.

'I wish it wasn't so dark in here,' I grumbled. 'I might have recognised those feet.'

Thrax wasn't listening. He lifted the lid from the cooking pot again, examined the alabastrons and finally picked one out. 'Nico,' he said, 'do you still have the jar that Fotini gave you?'

'Yes, it's in my bag.'

'Put it in here instead of this one.'

'Why, what's in that one?'

'Traces of poison, I believe. Nico, you can strike out clue number four from your list.'

CHAPTER 13

Toy Soldiers and Marbles

'That was Telephassa's cave, wasn't it?' I said. 'It's where she mixes her potions. That's what she had in the small basket. Alabastrons full of herbal potions to sell on the sly at the agora. Onatas knows nothing about her potion-making so she gets to keep the money she earns. Good on her.'

'She also makes poisons,' said Thrax.

Onatas was shutting the workshop as we came round the farmhouse. 'We might have to come back to have a look in there,' whispered Thrax.

'Pretend we've only just arrived, Nico. I need to speak with Onatas.'

'Good day, boys,' called Onatas, seeing us. 'Any news of Gorgias's ring?'

'Not yet, I'm afraid, sir,' said Thrax. 'We still need some more information. But we hope to conclude our investigations soon. Tell me, do you remember who you were sitting with at the symposium?'

'I was meant to share a couch with my brother-in-law, Ezekias,' replied Onatas. 'We always sit together when we're invited to the same party. But my nausea meant I had to stretch out and have the couch all to myself. Ezekias was brought a spare one.'

'You say Ezekias is your brother-in-law,' said Thrax.

'He married my only sister three years ago. But he was a close friend long before that. His parents owned a farm nearby. We used to play together, which is how he met my sister.'

'I take it Ezekias brought his slaves with him to the symposium.'

'He brought two of them,' said Onatas. 'Ezekias can be a bit of a show-off, especially if there are rich patrons he wants to impress. He's an olive merchant.'

'Do you think we could speak to him, sir?' asked Thrax. 'I need to find out more about those slaves.'

Onatas looked surprised by Thrax's request. 'He's in Athens for a few days, but perhaps my sister can help you.'

'Thank you, sir.'

Onatas wrote us a note and told us where to find Ezekias's house. 'You can't miss it,' he said. 'It's the third house along the street above the agora. There's a mosaic of Athena above the front door.'

We found Ezekias's house without any problems. A thick-set slave in a patterned chiton answered the door and told us to wait on the doorstep. A few moments later a very old woman came out. She had the end of her chiton drawn across her wrinkled face.

'Can I help you?' she said through the cloth.

'We want to speak to the lady of the house,' said Thrax. 'Onatas the sculptor sent us.'

'Wait here,' said the woman. The door closed on us once more. When it opened again, the old woman was smiling icily. 'Mistress says to come in.'

We followed her into a pretty courtyard with a pomegranate tree in the middle. A woman in her thirties came down the stairs.

'How can I help you, boys? Is anything wrong?'

'We are helping Master Onatas retrieve a missing ring,' said Thrax.

'Oh, you must be the talented mystery-solver my brother was talking about,' said the woman. 'Onatas has told us all about the theft. I am Helena. How can I help?'

'We need to speak to your slaves. The two male ones who went to the symposium with Master Ezekias on the night of the robbery. I believe one of them might have been involved without knowing it. But we mustn't make it look like we have come especially to talk to him. It might put him on his guard if he thinks he's in trouble.'

Helena's eyebrows arched in surprise. 'One of my slaves, involved in a robbery? Who'd have thought it? Come into the andron. It'll be all right to sit there while my husband is away.'

I was just as surprised as Helena to hear the thief might have had an accomplice, who might not have had any idea he was involved in a crime.

The slave who'd opened the door came in with cups and a jug. I threw a discreet glance at his feet. They were certainly the right size to fit in the sandal boots that had left the mysterious footprints in the workshop. He served the wine and bowed to his mistress before leaving.

'Well, was it him?' Helena demanded. 'He's capable of it, you know. He's robbed before and been punished for it.'

'You have no reason to punish him,' Thrax assured her.

The curtain to the andron parted again and a boy of about five or six came in with bowls of nuts. He put them down carefully on the table.

'This is Lampus,' said Helena.

Thrax smiled at the boy. 'Thank you, Lampus.'

The boy looked at Thrax in surprise. He was not used to being thanked.

'I see you like painting,' said Thrax.

Lampus's look of surprise turned to amazement.

'You have minute dots of paint on your arms and legs,' said Thrax. 'What have you been painting? Toy soldiers?'

Lampus nodded shyly. 'Spartans.'

'Iros, the older slave, carves them for him,' Helena explained. 'He's Lampus's father and a very gifted carver. Ezekias encourages him.'

'Nico and I would love to see your toy soldiers,' Thrax said to Lampus.

Lampus looked at Helena, who nodded. 'You may show our visitors.'

We followed the young slave out of the andron and across the yard. He opened a back door and we emerged into a shady lane, roofed over with a gnarled grapevine. Across it was a row of sheds. Some were stores for animal feed, others small workshops. Lampus showed us into one of them.

It was spotlessly clean and smelled of pigment and glue. A row of freshly painted soldiers stood drying on a windowsill.

'Ah,' said Thrax. 'This one here must be Odysseus himself. I can tell because he looks like a prince. And this one is Sinon, isn't he? The Greek soldier who pretended he'd been left behind in Troy. You've painted him very well, Lampus. Well done.'

Lampus grinned, pleased that Thrax had recognised the little figures.

'It's a pity you lost the horse to put the soldiers in,' said Thrax. 'Did you leave it somewhere?'

Lampus nodded. 'I took it with me to a symposium a few days ago. I must have left it there. But Father is going to make me a better one.'

'You must be more careful with your toys,' said Thrax gently. 'Have you got any others?'

Lampus went to a battered chest in the corner of the shed. It was covered in faded pictures of scenes from mythology: Herakles fighting the hydra; Perseus holding up Medusa's head and Pegasus swooping over a fire-breathing chimera. He threw back the lid to reveal a small collection of ragged toys. I realised he

must have been given them by kind friends of the family, or rescued them from rubbish heaps. Thrax lifted out a horse's head, made of cracked leather. It was stuck on a short pole and had only one eye.

'Ah, a hobby horse,' said Thrax. 'I always wanted one of these when I was younger. You're a very lucky boy. What else have you got in here? Have you got any marbles?'

'Yes.' Lampus picked up a stoppered jar and rattled it.

'Now, I think you've lost one of your marbles, haven't you?'

'Yes. It was inside the wooden horse when I lost it at the symposium. I like the rattling noise it makes when I pull the horse along.'

'It was a nice grey stone one, with white swirls going through it. A champion,' said Thrax. 'Well, I found a marble like that, although it wasn't in a wooden horse. I wonder if it's yours?'

He reached inside his bag and drew out the marble. It was the one from Onatas's tool chest. Lampus's face lit up and he reached for it.

'It is yours, isn't it?'

'Yes!' Lampus opened the clay jar and pushed the marble in with his finger. 'I'll never lose it again. I promise.'

'You can cross clue number two off your list,' grinned Thrax after we'd said goodbye to Helena. It was lunchtime, and we had stopped at the agora for something to eat.

There was only one clue left to tackle but I had to admit I had no idea how any of them fitted into the mystery. How had that marble moved out of Lampus's wooden horse and ended up in Onatas's tool chest?

'Hurry up, Nico,' said Thrax. 'Finish your food. I've solved the crime, but we have one more clue to find.'

'You mean you know who the thief is?'

'Yes, but I need to check one last thing before I reveal the name.'

'Clue number three,' I said. 'Keys.'

Thrax smiled. 'We're looking for two keys.'

'Where are you hoping to find them?'

'If my hunch is right, they are on Onatas's farm. 'Hiding in plain sight.'

I looked at Thrax in astonishment. 'You mean you have seen them already?'

Thrax smiled. 'And so have you. You just didn't know you were looking at them. To be honest, neither did I, till I had a good think.'

'And we're going to get them now?'

'Tonight,' said Thrax. 'We need the cover of darkness.'

CHAPTER 14

Spies in the Night

We returned to Inacus's house for clean chitons. Despite our best attempts to avoid Master Ariston, he waylaid us coming out of the kitchen.

'Inacus is having a little symposium tonight. Nothing grand, just me and two of his closest friends. We're going to show them how fast Hero is progressing at his orating skills. I'll need you both with me. Thrax, make sure my harp is in tune. I might, just might, sing one or two songs.'

The small city gate behind our street was locked by the time we were finally ready to leave.

'Come on,' said Thrax. 'We'll have to use the main gate.'

We crossed the city, which was still busy despite the late hour. The main gate was shut but not locked. Thrax pulled it open and we let ourselves through. We soon reached Onatas's farm and crouched behind the old carob tree to get our bearings.

Omega heard us and started barking madly. The door to Timon's hut opened. We saw the old slave outlined in the doorway. He stood there for what seemed like an eternity, peering through the darkness. Omega growled softly at his feet. But at last he dragged the dog back inside and we heard a bolt being drawn.

'Wait for me up in the tree, Nico,' whispered Thrax. 'And pray I don't alarm Omega again. I need to get really close to Timon's hut.'

He slipped out from behind the tree and I watched him running through the weeds. He stopped at the wooden figure of Hephaestus in the vegetable patch and removed something from it. I strained to see what it was, but there was not enough moonlight.

Thrax crossed over to the farmhouse, silent as a shadow. He must have found the door locked because he stepped back from the house and looked up at the slanting roof.

I looked on in awe as he scrambled up the wall, using the wide gaps between the mud bricks as footholds. Up on the roof he hesitated for a moment, then moved swiftly across and stopped. A faint glow illuminated his face and I knew that he was looking down a hole at a dying fire. He was standing directly above Telephassa's kitchen.

A moment later Thrax disappeared. He had leaped down into the house. I don't know how long I waited up there in the tree, my heart beating loudly, but at last I saw the farmhouse door open and close again. A shadow stole across the grass, heading straight for me.

'Nico!'

I gave him a hand up the tree. 'I take it everything went according to plan?'

He chuckled in the darkness. 'It did.'

'So what did you do in there, and in the vegetable patch? What did you remove from the bird scarer?'

'If I told you, it would spoil the surprise.'

I frowned. 'A surprise?'

'You don't have wait too long for it, I promise.'

We waited. The sky grew cobalt, then purple and finally red as dawn approached. Signs of life appeared in the farmhouse. Telephassa stomped out for firewood. Smilis hopped out to have a pee. Timon came out to milk the goats.

'Good morning, master,' he called to Onatas, who stepped out of the house yawning widely.

The sculptor crossed over to the workshop and fumbled at the keyring on his belt.

'What in the name of the gods…?'

Thrax dropped neatly out of the tree and ran over to the workshop. 'Can't you open the door, sir?'

'The stupid key won't turn in the lock.'

'Try this one,' said Thrax, producing a second key from his chiton. 'I think you'll find it fits.'

Onatas slipped Thrax's key in the lock. 'By Apollo's beard, it does. What does this mean, boy?'

'It means that I have solved the mystery, sir. I know who stole the ring.'

CHAPTER 15

Thrax Explains it All

Thrax and I were sat in Onatas's andron. After a long night in the tree, we were cold and starving. I welcomed the mound of tiganites Telephassa put before me.

While we ate, Onatas sent for Inacus, Gorgias and Master Ariston. They arrived almost together and joined us in the andron.

'Have you solved the mystery, boys?' asked Master Ariston, helping himself to tiganites. 'Tell us all about it.'

Gorgias leaned forward on the couch. 'Have you found the ring?

'Yes, sir,' said Thrax. 'I hope to have it for you in a moment.'

'Let him tell the story first, gentlemen,' said Onatas.

'As you all know, the ring of the harpies was stolen from Onatas's workshop five nights ago,' began Thrax. 'The thief managed to get into the workshop without breaking the door, unlocked the tool chest without a key, switched the ring for a child's marble and got out again, seemingly leaving no clues behind. I checked the workshop thoroughly and there really is no way in except through the door, and Onatas had the keys with him all the time. To the untrained eye, it seemed to be an impossible riddle.

'But even as we stood there, gawping in horror at the marble, I noticed that the thief had left a clue. A very big one.'

'And what was that clue?' asked Onatas.

'You told us, sir, that only us five here and your three slaves had been in the workshop that day. Three slaves, you, Master Ariston, Gorgias, Thrax and Nico. That meant there should have been eight sets of footprints in the marble dust but I detected a ninth set.

'Now my first reaction was that the thief had left them without knowing. But then I realised, surely someone who can get in and out of a locked door and steal a ring from a sealed chest, wouldn't be so stupid as to leave a set of footprints behind him?

'No, the prints had been left there on purpose, to mislead anyone who tried to investigate the crime. When I examined them carefully, I discovered they had been left by sandal boots. Cothurni. And there was something funny about them which raised my suspicions even further.'

'Something funny, you say?' exclaimed Master Ariston.

Thrax ignored him and went on. 'Now, Nico and I worked out that there were only three people who could have found out the ring was in the chest. Onatas had had no visitors to his workshop since the day he'd locked the ring in the box. So only the slaves could have known about it. Timon, Telephassa and Smilis. The thief had to be one of them, but they each had a witness to prove they were out of the house at the time the crime took place. Smilis and Timon were at a symposium with Onatas. Telephassa was at the sanctuary of Hekate till well after Onatas had come home. It seemed they were all in the clear. But, as in the case of most crimes, nothing is ever what it seems.

'Now back to the boots, the cothurni. Four days ago, we met Smilis on his way to deliver a basket of fish to Inacus. His feet were wet and there were tiny specks of pond weed stuck to his ankles. He claimed that he had been playing in the fountain in the agora. But fountains in market places never have weeds in them. They are cleaned regularly. And when we met Smilis, he wasn't coming from the direction of the market. He had just come out of an alleyway that led straight out of the city. There is a shrine to Demeter outside the city walls. People leave offerings of pomegranates on its altar. Smilis had pomegranate juice all over his face when

Nico and I met him. He'd stolen one of the fruits from the shrine. The little boy was lying. His feet had got wet somewhere other than the agora, somewhere outside the city. But why would he lie about such a trivial matter?

'I knew it had to be something to do with the crime, and it was. Nico and I discovered a large pond outside the city, past Demeter's shrine. It's well known for its freshwater fish and there was pond weed in it. Timon had sometimes taken Smilis there fishing, so the boy defintely knew about it. I found a pair of sandal boots drowned in the pond. There was a sliver of marble in the soles of one of them. Could it have come from Onatas's workshop, and could those sandals be the ones that were used to make the false footprints? Could the pond weed on Smilis's legs have come from here? If so, Smilis was definitely involved in the theft of the ring. But how? Was he working with someone else?

'Then I started thinking, what if one of the three slaves had actually left the place they were meant to be when the crime happened? Could Timon have sneaked out of the stables while making everyone believe he was still there? Did Telephassa leave the temple unnoticed only to creep back in after the crime had been committed? Could Smilis have left the symposium without Onatas knowing it? If so, how could they have done it?

'I racked my brains but could see no hint of a solution until Nico and I went to visit our friends Fotini and Gaia at the temple of Aphaia. We talked about poison, and suddenly I had it. I knew how the crime had been done, and by whom. I just needed proof to link the thief to the theft.'

'But what has poison got to do with it?' said Onatas. 'No one was poisoned.'

'Oh, but they were,' replied Thrax. 'Not enough to be killed, but enough to feel nauseous.'

Onatas looked at Thrax in horror. 'Do you mean me?'

'That mysterious nausea you suffered from at the symposium was caused by poison. Adder poison! It's not strong enough to kill you but it makes you terribly sick for a while.'

'But who poisoned me?' asked Onatas.

'At first I thought it might be Telephassa,' said Thrax. 'She makes poisons and herbal remedies. But then I realised it was someone else.'

Thrax looked at Onatas. 'Sir, I am a slave myself and I know that despair can make a person act irrationally. If I tell you how the crime was committed and who did it, will you promise to forgive? I do not yet know exactly what motive the thief had for stealing the ring but I think he was put under extreme pressure to do it. He might not have had a choice.'

There was a long silence while Onatas ruminated. 'Very well,' he said at last. 'I will not take any steps against the person who stole the ring, as long as it is returned. Who did it, then?'

'It was Smilis,' said Thrax.

Smilis? Everyone looked dumbfounded.

'The boy might act dumb but he is actually very clever,' said Thrax. 'Very few people would know so much about poison. Perhaps he has learnt a lot from Telephassa. It's a pity he's not a free man. He would make a great politician when he grows up. This is what happened.

'Someone approached Smilis and told him that Onatas had bought the ring of the harpies. Somehow they convinced him to steal it.'

'But who?' asked Master Ariston.

'And how did he know where I'd hidden the ring?' Onatas wanted to know.

'Smilis models for you, sir. He is very good at standing still. He has learned to spy on you by pretending to be a statue. It's a secret game he likes playing. There is a plinth in your workshop marked Eros. I found footprints on it. They were too faint for me to see properly but the feet that made them had been caked in flour. You sometimes get Smilis to dust himself in flour when he is modelling for you, don't you?'

'Yes,' answered Onatas. 'It makes him look like a marble statue and it gives me a better idea of what I am aiming for.'

'The day you put the ring in the tool chest, Smilis was pretending to be a statue. You didn't see him, but he saw everything you did.

'On the day of the theft, he put enough poison in your wine cup to make you nauseous. He stole the poison from Telephassa. Yesterday, Nico and I witnessed him returning the alabastron to her cave. Here it is. You'll find traces of poison in it. You'll find his finger marks on it too, from the honey cakes you two were eating outside the workshop.'

'But if that alabastron could incriminate the fellow, why wait so long to get rid of it?' asked Onatas.

'As I said, he took the jar from Telephassa, sir. She would eventually have noticed the theft if Smilis had not returned it. Perhaps the boy helps her with her potion-making and she knows he has access to the alabastrons. I'm sure he wanted to return it sooner but he had to wait for Telephassa to be out, making her weekly trip to the agora, before he could sneak into her cave unnoticed.

'And I think Smilis followed us when we retrieved the cothurni from the pond. He knew we might start to suspect him. He must have been desperate to get rid of the jar.'

'I can't believe the little rascal poisoned me,' said Onatas.

'You became nauseous and felt sick all through the symposium, sir,' continued Thrax. 'That is what Smilis wanted. While your mind was wandering, he switched the keys to the workshop and the tool chest on your ring with two other ones, old discarded ones that your bird scarer wears as earrings.'

Onatas stared. 'So when I couldn't open the workshop door this morning…'

'I had done the same as him, to prove to myself that it could be done. I removed the keys from the bird scarer's ears and sneaked into your house while you were sleeping. You never even felt me switching the keys.'

'But I swear by the gods that he never left my side at the symposium. He was fanning me all night long.'

'He switched places with your brother-in-law's slave, Lampus. I think he gave him a hobby horse as payment. You were in so much agony, sir, you never noticed it was Lampus fanning you and not Smilis.'

Onatas slapped his thigh. 'Smilis does have a hobby horse.'

'I think you'll find it in Lampus's possession now, sir. He is also the owner of the marble we found in your tool chest, which you passed on to me. It was taken from him at the symposium. I returned it to the boy myself.'

'So what you're saying is,' said Inacus, 'that Smilis switched places with Lampus, who kept fanning Onatas while Smilis ran all the way back to the workshop, opened the door with a key he'd stolen from his master, opened the tool chest, stole the ring, closed the chest and the door behind him and returned to the symposium, where he switched the keys again.'

'Unbelievable,' said Master Ariston. 'The boy is very clever indeed.'

'But how can you be sure it was him?' asked Inacus.

'It all goes back to the footprints,' said Thrax. 'Do you remember I told you the mysterious footprints didn't look right, Nico? The heels were far apart from each other and the toes close together. They are the kind of footprints a child wearing an adult's shoes would make.' He opened his bag and took out the cothurni we had recovered from the pond. 'Nico and I dried these very carefully. As you know sir, marble dust is more like grit. The particles have very sharp edges that embed themselves in soft material, especially if pressed down hard. Not even a long soaking in water can displace them. You'll find marble dust footprints inside the boots. They were made by Smilis when he stole the ring.'

'Where did Smilis get these boots from?' wondered Onatas.

'I expect he stole them, sir. Or he might have found them somewhere.'

'But where is the ring now?' asked Gorgias. 'Where did the rascal hide it?'

'In the most famous hiding place in history,' answered Thrax. 'Smilis also stole a wooden horse from Lampus at the symposium. A model of the wooden horse of Troy. The ring is inside it.'

CHAPTER 16

Melinoe

Just then we heard a crash outside the door. Thrax leaped off the couch and bolted out to the yard. I followed, only to find my eyes dazzled by the fierce sun. But even then I could see that the back door at the other end of the yard was wide open.

'It's Smilis,' said Thrax. 'He's running away.'

We both charged through the open door. Outside we could see the slave boy tearing down the hill, clutching the wooden horse under one arm. We charged after him, shouting 'good day' to the guard as we raced though the city gate.

Ahead of us, Smilis reached the end of the alley and turned left. We followed to see him disappear in the rubble of the ruined house in our street. By the time we got there ourselves, there was no sign of him. He seemed to have vanished.

'He's hiding somewhere,' I said. 'Perhaps he's discovered our secret meeting place.'

Thrax started towards the hut but I grabbed his arm. 'Look.'

I pointed to the statue of Melinoe. An adder was slithering around its feet and, just as in my nightmare, there was a head on the broken neck. The statue glared at me with large, malevolent eyes. I felt my skin crawl.

Thrax nudged me in the ribs. 'Come on, Nico. Can't you guess where Smilis went? He's getting away.'

He ran up to the statue and, ignoring the hissing snake, plunged two fingers in the statue's eyes. The eyeballs disappeared and the whole shrine swung sideways, revealing a doorway in the wall.

A secret tunnel.

Thrax plunged in, and I followed, steeling myself to get past the adder, which was now baring its fangs. I wished I still had Fotini's antidote, just in case. The shrine swung back into place behind me. Now we were in total darkness. The smell of damp was overpowering and the walls so close, my shoulders scraped against them. The ground was slippery underfoot. It was impossible to run.

'I wasn't having a nightmare the other night after all,' I said to Thrax. 'The statue of Melinoe did have a head.'

'It's a lever. You slot the head on the broken neck and poke the goddess in the eyes to open the door. Ingenious.'

'That ghostly figure I saw hovering near the shrine must have been real then too.'

'But not an actual shade,' said Thrax. 'A flesh and bones person coming out of the secret tunnel.'

I could feel rancid water dripping from the roof and running down my back as I followed Thrax. Bats shrieked in the darkness ahead. After a while the tunnel widened and the stench of damp was replaced by a briny smell. I felt a cool breeze on my face. The tunnel was leading us to the sea.

Up ahead we saw sunlight twinkling through a curtain of vivid green. For a moment Smilis was silhouetted against it but then it parted and he disappeared outside.

We stumbled after him through a layer of hanging weeds, out into rosy afternoon sunlight. An ancient sea wall stretched out in front of us, carved out of jagged black rocks. Sheer cliffs towered above us. It was a desolate place, the only sound the shrill cry of seagulls nesting in the rocks.

There was a ship docked at the sea wall. It was a hulking trireme, painted all black, its one sail furled up tight against the mast. It seemed to be completely deserted except for a lookout who was asleep at the prow.

There was no sign of Smilis.

'That ship is waiting for Smilis to deliver the ring,' said Thrax.

'But he stole it nearly five days ago. Why wait till now to deliver it?'

'There's a new moon tonight,' answered Thrax. 'Look, it's already in the sky. It must be the signal for their meeting. Pirates often conduct important business on the night of a new moon. They think it brings them good luck.'

I stared at the hulking trireme. 'You mean that's a pirate ship?'

'Don't you recognise it?' said Thrax. 'There are no eyes on the prow. It's the same vessel that tried to skewer us on our way to Aegina.'

'That means the captain on board is the pirate with the golden mask. I wonder how he got to know about the ring of the harpies, and how he got in touch with Smilis.'

'We need to find Smilis before he gets on board that ship,' I said. 'They'll be sure to sell him off when they have no more use of him. Pirates are notorious for selling children to slave traders.'

We searched all over the shore but failed to find the slave boy. In the end, we found a shady spot where we could keep a lookout. Slowly, the hot day faded into a balmy evening. The sky grew dark. Finally, there was movement on the ship. A dark figure rose out of the deck, followed promptly by another.

'The pirate with the golden mask,' I gasped.

'And his henchman, the pirate with the silver mask,' added Thrax. 'He's waving a torch. Oh no! Nico, look.'

Smilis had crept up to the ship unnoticed and was clambering over the bulwarks, the wooden horse still clamped firmly under one arm. The pirate in the silver mask came forward. He took the boy by the hand and led him to the stern, where the pirate in the golden mask had appeared. There was a grating noise, and the three of them sunk below deck. The ship appeared deserted once more.

'That boy has no idea what danger he's in,' said Thrax. 'Come on. We can't abandon him now.' Within moments he had scurried down to the quay. I ran after him but he reached the ship before me and, using the oar holes as footholds, climbed over the bulwarks.

Thrax reached down to me. 'Come on, Nico, I'll pull you up.'

Somehow I managed to hit the deck without twisting my ankle. The ship swayed lightly under my feet and I thanked the gods it was a calm evening. I always get sick on choppy waters, even in a harbour.

'What now, Thrax?' I asked.

He pointed to a stack of amphorae under the mast. 'We hide behind those.'

We squatted behind the jars, keeping our heads low. Sitting there, I thought I could hear a faint moaning sound coming from below. It's the kind of noise I imagined the shades on Charon's boat would make. It made my skin crawl.

CHAPTER 17

The Discus Thrower

'Can you hear that?' I asked Thrax.

'Hear what?'

'Moaning.'

Thrax listened. 'I can't hear any moaning.'

I put my ear to the planking. But now the moaning had stopped. Instead, I could hear proper voices. I signalled to Thrax and he put his ear to the deck too.

'I pray our trust in you was not in vain.'

'No, sir,' replied a weaker voice. 'I have the ring, sir.' It was Smilis.

'So what are you waiting for? Give it to me.'

There was a rattling sound and I imagined Smilis shaking the ring out of the trapdoor in the wooden horse's belly. Then a pause, and finally a deep, satisfied sigh. 'Aaah, at last. The ring is mine.'

We heard footsteps and then the three figures rose out of the deck again. Peeping from behind the amphorae, I saw the pirate in the golden mask put the ring on his finger. He held it up to the moonlight. It sparkled, and the eyes of the winged monsters glowed like embers.

'I am glad you like it, sir,' said Smilis. 'Perhaps now I can claim my reward?'

The pirate in the golden mask chuckled deep in his throat. 'Your reward?'

'Your man promised me that if I got you the ring, you would take me away with you on the high seas. That you'd teach me to become a pirate like yourself.'

Hideous laughter echoed from the silver mask and I recognised it at once. Belos! My mind reeled at the thought. Had he run away to sea?

'He promised me, in the name of Melinoe,' insisted Smilis.

'You little fool,' growled Belos. 'Melinoe is the mother of cheats. You've been had.' He turned to the taller man beside him. 'Shall I throw him in with the others, sir?'

The pirate in the golden mask nodded. Smilis, realising he was in danger, hurled the wooden horse at Belos, hitting the silver mask full on. Belos cried out in pain, then leaped at Smilis. But the slave boy squirmed out of his grasp. He got to the bulwarks and vaulted over them. I looked down, expecting to see Smilis sprawled out on the quay, but he had landed on his feet. He stuck out his tongue cheekily at Belos and ran towards the tunnel.

He didn't get very far. The taller pirate unhooked the golden mask from his face and hurled it like a discus.

It hit Smilis squarely in the heel and sent him sprawling to the ground, like the hero Achilles felled by an arrow. I looked, thunderstruck, from the golden mask lying on the quay back to the pirate. He was swiftly pulling his himation over his head.

But he hadn't been quick enough. I caught a fleeting glimpse of his face before the himation hid it from view. The pirate in the golden mask was our bitterest enemy.

Abantes, the crooked priest from Delphi!

CHAPTER 18

Prisoners

Thrax and I had crossed swords with Abantes in Delphi, where he was one of the priests working in the famous oracle. We had caught him accepting bribes to change the Pythia's message, a heinous crime that could have ruined the reputation of the oracle. The last time I'd seen him, he was threatening to have revenge on Thrax and me.

Now here we were, hiding on his ship.

Myrmidons swarmed off the trireme and surrounded Smilis, jabbing at him with their spears. Two of them hauled him to his feet and dragged him back to the ship. A third retrieved the golden mask and returned it to its owner.

Abantes put the mask back on his face and pulled down his himation. He inspected his reflection in a mirror, which Belos had brought from the stern where a lamp burned in front of a statue of Poseidon. 'Tie up the little fool and throw him in the hold with the others.'

Smilis was dragged away, kicking and screaming. A moment later I felt the sharp tip of a myrmidon's spear in the small of my back. 'Put your hands above your head and get up, both of you.'

I stood slowly, coming into full view of Abantes and Belos.

'By the gods,' exclaimed Belos. 'Look what the mighty Poseidon has spat on to our ship, Father.'

Abantes's eyes glared at me with pure hatred through the peepholes of his golden mask. 'It is not Poseidon who has delivered the fools into our hands. It is my immeasurable desire for revenge. Hate, my son, is stronger than faith in the gods.

Remember that.' He held up his right hand for Thrax and myself to see.

'Are you still looking for this? You will never lay your hands on it, nor return it to that boor of a merchant, Gorgias. I have wanted this ring ever since his weakling of a son told me about it. And when my spies told me that the merchant had tasked you with finding it for him, my desire for it grew even more. Look how perfectly it fits my finger. It belongs there.'

He waggled his fingers so that the ring caught the moonlight and flashed like a star. The harpies' eyes glowed even brighter. 'I imbue this ring with all my anger and hatred…'

'Your threats do not scare us,' Thrax cut in. 'People may quake at the sound of your name but we know you to be a fake and a charlatan. What are you? A priest, a pirate, a retired naval officer?'

'I am all three,' hissed Abantes. 'I led a double life as a navy officer and a pirate for a long time. And lately I have also been a priest. Not out of love for the gods but because it brought me a lot of power and respect.'

'We will take the ring back from you,' said Thrax. 'Only we won't be stealing it. We'll be claiming it in the name of Gorgias, who will give it to his niece. She inherited it from her father.'

Abantes growled through the mask. 'Get them out of my sight before I run them through with my dagger.'

'But you have revealed our identity to them, Father,' protested Belos. 'They must die or they will give us away.'

'It will not matter,' replied Abantes. 'This is the last voyage of the ship with no eyes. I am giving up the sea. You and I shall retire to a place so remote, not even the gods will find us. We will live in splendour on our ill-gotten gains. As for these two, we shall trade them on with the others.'

Two of the myrmidons grabbed us and tied our hands tightly together. We were dragged across the deck towards a trapdoor and shoved down a short flight of stairs.

At once, I could hear that spooky moaning sound again. It grew louder as the myrmidons hauled us to a second trapdoor and dropped us like sacks into the deepest part of the ship, the hold. I landed face down in a handspan of dirty bilge water. The haunting noise stopped for a moment and I heard a loud gasp before it started again, louder than ever. I realised my imagination hadn't been playing tricks on me after all. The eerie noise was real. There were children imprisoned in this ship and they were all moaning.

The trapdoor crashed shut and the darkness wrapped around me like a shroud, tight and suffocating. The air reeked of sweat and pee. I managed to get to my feet, only to bang my head against the low ceiling.

'Grapes,' sobbed someone – a girl I think, although it could have been a boy, faint with hunger – over my shoulder. 'Do you have any grapes? My mother always gives me grapes before I go to bed.'

'I have no food on me,' I said, rubbing my sore head with my tied-up hands. 'Not even a grape.'

'Nico,' said Thrax. 'Clear your mind and concentrate. We must find a way out of here.'

'Yes,' I agreed. 'We need a plan. Where do you think this ship is heading?'

'To an island somewhere in Megale Hellas,' said a girl who was squashed in between Thrax and a very small boy. 'I overheard the rowers talking about it the last time we were allowed on deck. They are exchanging us for salt.'

Megale Hellas was a vast region at the western end of the Hellenic world. People from Hellas had settled there hundreds of years ago, taking with them a sacred flame from the mother country to light the fires in the new temples. They founded colonies that grew into rich and powerful cities. It's somewhere I'd always dreamed of visiting, but not in chains.

'How many of you are imprisoned in this ship?' Thrax asked the girl.

'We were nine before they brought you two and the other boy in.'

'That makes twelve of us,' said Thrax.

'Twelve against thirty rowers, a gang of myrmidons, a helmsman, a piper and two madmen,' I said. 'We're going to need a really good plan if we are to escape.'

'We will escape,' Thrax assured me. 'I have no intention of being exchanged for a pot of salt. And I mean to take the ring of the harpies with me when I leave this ship.'

CHAPTER 19

Alexa

The trireme lurched suddenly, throwing everyone off their feet. Some of the children screamed and most started wailing again. A few kicked against the hull with their bare feet. We were on the move.

'Where's Smilis?' I asked Thrax.

By now our eyes had grown used to the dark and we spotted him sitting alone with his back against the hull. I waved at him with my bound hands but he looked away.

Thrax called out to the children. 'Silence, everyone. Sit down quietly. If you spread out there's plenty of room for us all. My name is Thrax. This is my friend Nico and that boy over there who was brought in just before us is Smilis. He's my friend too. We're going to escape and we'll take anyone who wants to come with us. How many of you would like to leave this ship?'

All the children except Smilis nodded. My heart went out to him. I wished I could put my arms round him and tell him I understood why he'd stolen the ring. If I were a young boy with only a slave's bitter future ahead of me, I too might have been tempted to steal from my master.

Thrax must have been thinking the same as me. 'Smilis,' he called, 'shall I count you in with us? Nico and I are going to need your help.'

Smilis turned his face to the wall but nodded.

'Good,' said Thrax. 'Now listen, everyone. I calculate it will take at least six days to get to our destination. Our ship will sail at night, to avoid running into Athenian or Aeginian ships. During the day, the pirates will drop anchor in some secret bay or harbour. But after two or three days we'll have to strike out into open waters till we get to Megale Hellas. So we have only a few nights when we'll still be close enough to land to escape.'

He turned to the girl next to him. 'You said you are sometimes allowed on deck.'

'Every morning when the ship docks,' replied the girl, whose name was Alexa. 'But only for a short while. It's to let us breathe some fresh air and to drink. They give us food too; a small crust of stale bread to make sure we're worth our salt when they come to barter us. The rowers and the myrmidons go ashore to offer sacrifice and raid hamlets and farms. But one of them always stays behind to stand guard over us. Not that we can even think about escaping! Our hands are tied all the time.'

'What about the pirates in the gold and silver masks?' asked Thrax. 'Do they go ashore too?'

'Yes,' replied Alexa. 'But they don't stay with the crew. They go further inland, alone. Some say they go to drink the blood of innocent children.'

'Ha,' said Thrax. 'A likely story. Now listen carefully. When we're let out in the morning, I need someone to distract the guard. I have something really important to do.'

'I could pretend I've fainted with hunger,' said Alexa. 'That always has the guard worried. The pirate in the golden mask is very keen to get as much salt for us as possible.'

'Or I could pretend I'm sick from drinking bilge water,' I suggested.

'Let's try that, Nico,' said Thrax. 'If it doesn't work, Alexa can pretend to faint from hunger.

He patted Alexa on the shoulder and I noticed that his hands were free.

'Thrax,' I gasped. 'How did you do that?'

He laughed. 'I held my wrists slightly apart when the myrmidon tied my hands. It gave the rope some slack. Look, I can slip my hands in and out of the knot as I please.'

I stared at him in admiration. 'Thrax, I do believe you'll get us off this ship and back to Aegina after all.'

The night passed very slowly and by morning I was frantic to be let out and gulp down some fresh air. We all scrambled to our feet, slipping in pee and bilge water, as one of the myrmidons pulled open the trapdoor. Rough hands reached down to haul us up one by one.

'Follow me,' said a myrmidon who, I guessed, was going to be looking after us while the rest went ashore. He fixed Thrax and I with a glare. 'And no tricks from either of you two. Try and jump into the sea and I'll spear you like a fish.'

We tramped in single file up to the deck. The sun was just about to rise and the air smelled fresh and invigorating. I breathed in deep to clear out my lungs. We had docked in a rocky cove surrounded by steep cliffs. There was a wide crack down the middle of them, forming a dark path into a green forest.

An altar stood on the rocks close to the shore, where the crew was offering sacrifice. I'd heard that sailors often drown horses in honour of the sea god but this lot was only burning fruit and pouring wine on the altar. Abantes and Belos were nowhere to be seen. Perhaps they'd gone inland already, through the path in the cliffs.

'Walk around the deck,' ordered the myrmidon. 'Get some strength back into your legs. Single file.'

Thrax was at the other end of the line, near the stern, as we started marching up and down the ship. He seemed to be edging towards a small altar with a statue of Poseidon on it. I glimpsed a fishing boat far out at sea and wished I could wave to get the crew's attention. Alexa nudged me in the ribs with her elbow and we launched into our planned diversion. I crumpled up my face and howled loudly in pain.

'What's the matter?' asked Alexa, pretending to look concerned.

'My stomach. Aargh… Aargh… I shouldn't have drunk that bilge water. I'm going to throw up.'

The myrmidon, who'd marched up to see why I was causing a fuss, took a hurried step backwards. 'Don't you dare throw up on my

clean deck or I'll make you mop it up with your own tongue.'

'I can't help it, sir,' I moaned. 'Oh, it feels like the hydra itself is tearing my insides apart.'

'Well, be sick in the sea if you have too,' snapped the myrmidon. 'Get moving.'

I stumbled to the bulwark, followed by Alexa, and made loud gagging noises over the side. I kept it up till my throat was so dry, it hurt.

'Thank you, sir,' I said to the myrmidon when I couldn't retch any more. 'I feel better now.'

The myrmidon who had been handing out the bread glared at me. 'Get back in line, then.'

I threw a sideways glance at Thrax as I took my place with the others. Somehow he had managed to get hold of Abantes's mirror. He was holding it up to catch the ligh of the rising sun.

I realised what he was doing right away. He was signalling to someone out at sea. But who?

CHAPTER 20

A Friend to the Rescue

'That was a risky thing to do, Thrax,' I said. 'Thank the gods you weren't caught.'

'I had my back to the shore,' he said. 'No one could have seen me signalling.'

We were in the hold again. Despite the stench, my stomach rumbled with hunger. I'd missed out on my rations and I wouldn't get anything to eat till the next day.

Alexa pulled a small hunk of bread from inside her chiton. 'I saved you some,' she said.

Thrax and I shared the bread between us, eating slowly to make it last.

'Who were you signalling to, Thrax?' I asked.

As usual, I didn't get a proper answer. 'It's best not to talk about it before my plan bears fruit. Why don't you tell the children a story to pass the time? Perhaps you could tell them about our adventure in Corinth last year.'

And, sitting in that stinking hold, I performed in public for the very first time. It wasn't the luxurious andron filled with important patrons I had dreamed about, but it was a great success. My young audience lapped it up and they rapped against the hull in my honour when I finished.

Not long afterwards we felt the ship tremble and heard the oars cutting through the water. We were on the move again. I had spent the entire day telling my story.

Next morning, we anchored once more. This time we had docked in a natural harbour. Gentle hills sloped down towards it. They were covered in ancient olive trees, the remains of a sacred grove. I could tell people still came here to honour the spirits of the trees. They had left scarlet ribbons fluttering in the branches.

We marched endlessly between the prow and the stern while our guard barked out encouragement and the rest of the crew lugged heavy stones from the water to a spot among the gnarled olive trees. They were building an altar.

The sun rose higher in the sky. The cicadas shrilled in the trees. It got face-burningly hot and my head swam. A fight for bread broke out among the children and I wished my hands were free so I could block out the noise.

My knees began to hurt from all the marching and I was almost glad when the myrmidon on duty counted us down into the hold. I leaned against the hull, sweaty and breathless.

'Shall I tell you another story?' I said to the others, to keep my mind off my pitiful state. 'Thrax and I had a marvellous adventure in Delphi.'

'We'd like to hear about it,' chirped a girl nearby. I jumped when I heard that voice. The girl was as tall as Alexa and had the same flowing hair. But it wasn't Alexa. It was Fotini.

She grinned when she saw the look on my face. 'Hello, Nico.'

I struggled to get the words out. 'Fotini! How… how did you get in here?'

'I swapped places with Alexa. Remember when you came to see me at the temple, I said I was worried for your safety? Well, after you left I hired some men from the temple to shadow you and report back to me. They followed you to Onatas's house and then along the tunnel behind the shrine of Melinoe. Did you know that ruined house used to belong to Abantes before he was exiled? He must have used it to get to his pirate ship while he was still a respected naval office in Aegina. My spies told me all about it. The authorities in Aegina pulled the house down as punishment when he was caught stealing from a temple. I guessed from my spies' descriptions that he and Belos were the men who kidnapped you.'

'Ha,' I said. 'I saw a ghostly figure outside the shrine to Melinoe. It gave me nightmares.'

'That must have been one of Abantes's minions,' said Fotini. 'My men tell me the city is full of them. They must have been getting ready for their master's return. It's pure luck they didn't find out about you.'

'But how did you follow us once we'd set sail?' I asked.

Fotini giggled. 'When you were captured on this trireme, I hired a large fishing boat and started tailing you. I thought I'd lost you for a while but Thrax flashed me a message across the sea yesterday morning and we picked up your trail again. And now I have come to your rescue.'

'I spotted your boat,' I said, 'but I couldn't find a way to signal. And how did you get on board?'

'When you docked this morning, my men hid the fishing boat round the headland and I swam here. I brought a rope with me so I could climb up the hull. You didn't see me, Nico, but Thrax did and he created a diversion.'

'The quarrel over the bread?' I said.

Thrax smiled. 'It gave Fotini time to cut the rope around Alexa's hands and swap places with her.'

I turned to Thrax. 'If you signalled to Fotini, you must have known she was following us.'

'I didn't know for sure if she was on that fishing boat,' said Thrax. 'But I had a feeling she might be.'

I looked at Fotini in pure admiration. She was taking a terrible risk, pretending to be a prisoner. If we didn't manage to get off this ship before we reached Megale Hellas, she would be exchanged for a bag of salt instead of Alexa. I shook the horrific thought from my head. I needed to believe we could save ourselves. We were the Medusa League after all. We had outwitted thieves and murderers. We would outwit pirates too. I prayed to the gods my hopes would come true.

'And where is Alexa now?' I asked Fotini.

'Hiding somewhere on the fishing boat, waiting to help us,' said Fotini, fingering the Medusa League medallion around her neck. 'Thrax, what's your plan?'

Thrax looked from Fotini to me. 'Did you look at the altar the myrmidons are building on the shore? It's for a special festival in honour of Poseidon. The people of Aegina have a sixteen-day festival for the god every year. People who work out at sea often miss it, so they have their own little festival. It only lasts a night but it is enough to ensure Poseidon's blessing for the whole year.'

'The priestess at the temple told me about this festival,' chipped in Fotini. 'You must have noticed that the crew is using only black stones to build the altar. That's because the special altar for the festival has to be jet black, like Poseidon's dark home at the bottom of the sea. It reminds the sailors of their ancestors hiding inside the Trojan horse too. Men from Aegina fought in the Trojan War and they believe Poseidon helped them home across the sea. They started this festival to thank him.'

'I hope they're not sacrificing a horse,' I said.

'They don't have one,' said Thrax. 'And even if they did, Abantes would not let them sacrifice something as precious as a horse. I don't think he really believes in gods and goddesses. He only takes part in rituals to impress people.'

'So are we going to try and escape during the festival? I asked.

Thrax nodded. 'Listen carefully. This is what we have to do…'

CHAPTER 21

The Festival of Poseidon

Time in the hold passed slowly, as it always does when you have nothing to do except wait. But at last we could hear a myrmidon tramping down from the deck. He rattled the bolt on the trapdoor to make sure it was securely drawn. We all held our breath as his footsteps receded and we could hear the thump of his boots against the outside of the hull. He was climbing down to join his colleagues on the shore.

We waited a bit longer, to make sure he was gone, then Fotini got up, careful not to bang her head against the low ceiling. 'It will take me only a short while to find the herbs for the potion. It is an easy one to make, assuming I can find a spring of fresh water. The potion is very powerful but it will not work with seawater. I have an alabastron to carry it in. I'll make sure it's a strong one so that it will take effect on the men very quickly. I suggest one of you keeps a lookout to make sure everything goes according to plan. If I get caught, try to find another way to escape.'

'Nico and I will both come up on deck with you,' Thrax said. 'Nico especially is becoming very good at being a lookout.' Fotini passed him a small dagger, which he used to cut the rope around my wrists. The other children saw it and crowded round, holding out their bound hands. Thrax obliged, smiling. 'Listen, everyone, my friends and I are trying to get you off this horrible ship. You must sit here patiently and wait. But be ready to go when we come for you. Smilis, I am leaving you in charge.'

He banged on the trapdoor with the flat of his hand. A few moments later the bolt was drawn and I saw Alexa's anxious face peering down at us. Fotini hauled herself up first. 'Good luck,' I whispered after her. She turned and smiled before the darkness swallowed her.

Thrax and I followed, Thrax going first so he could give me a hand up. We stole up to the deck and soon found a vantage point behind the pile of amphorae. It was cloudy but the night was still bright enough to let us observe the men on the seashore.

I could see two dark heads bobbing in the surf. Fotini had taken Alexa with her, to help make the potion. I prayed no one on the shore would notice them or hear them splashing as they got out of the water. The men had formed a ring around the altar, Abantes towering above them in his golden mask. I guessed he was standing on a large stone, to mark him out as Poseidon's ambassador for the ritual. There was a large stamnos at one end of the altar. A statue of Poseidon stood at the other end, facing out to sea.

Belos, wearing a scaly mask to show he was playing the part of Triton, Poseidon's beloved son, dragged a bleating goat to be sacrificed. The men hauled it on to the altar stone, holding it down while Abantes recited a prayer to the god. He sprinkled it with something from a lekythos and I knew this to be sacred salt, which is always used in grand rituals. Then he raised a knife high above its head and brought it down on the goat.

His voice rang across the water. 'Behold, the power of Poseidon is strong on land and sea. He maketh the waves, he maketh the salt.'

The men piled driftwood around the slaughtered animal and set it alight. The acrid stench of burning flesh filled the air.

Abantes carried the statue of Poseidon down to the water's edge with the men following and chanting. They thrust their hands inside their chitons to pull out bits of stale bread, which they threw into the sea as offerings.

'I heard a priest tell about this at a symposium,' I said to Thrax. 'They are feeding the fish in the hope that they will tell Poseidon how generous

they are. In return, they pray Poseidon will be kind to them as they travel across the surface of his kingdom.'

Behind the men, a small dark shape slipped out from among the olive trees. It was Fotini. She peered around to make no one had seen her and ran to the altar, where she poured her potion into the stamnos.

'Perfectly done,' said Thrax.

Slowly, the smell of flesh and goat's hair turned into the delicious aroma of roasting meat. The men returned from the edge of the water and Belos handed out drinking cups. His father carved the meat and the men grabbed it by the handful. I had expected a noisy banquet with dancing and wild games but the men all dined alone, each one sitting by themselves on the sand.

'Our plan is working. Nico, watch,' whispered Thrax.

As I looked on in amazement, Abantes's head started to droop to his chest. The wine cup slipped out of his hands and fell in the sand. All around him, myrmidons and rowers were falling asleep too. Their loud snoring carried across the sea.

Fotini had spiked the wine with a powerful sleeping potion.

CHAPTER 22

Escape

Thrax got to his feet. 'Wait for me here, Nico. This won't take long. We'll free the children as soon as I get back.'

He removed his chiton, hopped on the bulwarks and dived neatly into the sea. I watched him strike out towards the shore. Once there, he sprinted towards Abantes, who was slumped over the altar. Carefully, he removed the ring of the harpies from the pirate's finger and slipped it on his own. Abantes snorted in his sleep but didn't wake up. Thrax backed away from the altar. Then he turned and ran to the sea.

I helped him back over the bulwarks.

The ring of the harpies glinted in the moonlight. The harpies' golden wings shone. Their eyes glowed a bright red. They were made from a special stone called carnelian, but in that moment they looked almost real. I realised I was looking at a true work of art, a priceless treasure.

'Put it in your bag for safekeeping, Nico,' said Thrax, slipping it off his finger. 'A slave has no use for jewellery. Now let's go and free those children. We need to get away from here before the men come round.'

Below deck, he threw open the trapdoor. The children were huddled under it, waiting in complete silence. We pulled them up one by one.

'Aphrodite... Jacob... Dido... Miletus...'

Many had names from faraway countries and I wondered if they would ever make it home to their families, to their loved ones.

'Now follow us,' said Thrax. 'We need to be fast, and we need to concentrate.'

Fotini's men had rowed the fishing boat up to the trireme. We lowered the children down into their arms and they set them down on the planking. With everyone on board, we rowed away from the cove and out to the open sea.

Fotini introduced us to the crew of the fishing boat – Captain Theopompos and his sons, Carpus and Castor, who were both busy hoisting up the sail.

'How long will it take to get back to Aegina?' asked Thrax.

'Just two days and two nights, if Eurus, the god of the east wind, favours us. We'll need to stop and hide for the night, though, or we might fall in the clutches of some other pirate.'

Eurus did indeed bless our little boat. His enchanted breath filled our sail and we made good progress, leaving Abantes and Belos far behind. At the end of the day we stopped at a small island where Theopompos assured us we would find water to drink and wild fruit to eat.

To my surprise, he ordered Carpus and Castor to take down the sail. The mast was then removed from its moorings and the ship hoisted up into the branches of a tree.

'Ha,' remarked Theopompos, stepping back and squinting up at the foliage. 'You can't see the boat from here, let alone from out at sea. We'll be safe from pirates tonight.'

After a dinner of figs and spring water, Thrax, Fotini and I clambered up into another tree to sleep, while the children lay in the tall grass, cosy under himations the fishermen had lent them. Soon they were all fast asleep. Looking down at them, I thought how small and vulnerable they looked. None of them could have been over eight and I wondered if their mothers still hoped they would come home one day, safe and sound.

Then I thought of Abantes. He would have woken up at dawn to find the ring of the harpies had vanished and his precious cargo of young slaves gone. I was sure he would follow us and I prayed that we would get back safely to Aegina before he caught up with us.

I never wanted to see the ship with no eyes again.

CHAPTER 23

The Jaws of Charybdis

I woke up before dawn and helped the fishermen manoeuvre the boat down from the tree. The sea was smooth as a polished mirror as we sailed away, our chitons bulging with fruit for the journey. But shortly after the sixth hour of the day, Eurus abandoned us, leaving our boat at the mercy of his wilder brother Notus.

Notus is believed to be especially cruel at the end of summer, when he likes to flood the autumn crops and whips the sea up into horrific storms. He was churning up a storm around us now, as we sailed past a small peninsula.

The sky darkened with rain clouds. The sea started to heave and soon our little ship was being thrown about like a dice in a gambler's cup. Rain pelted down, soaking us through and making the children cry out in panic. Theopompos furled up the sail and ordered Corpus and Castor to row for the nearest coast.

They'd hardly pulled out the oars when I spotted a dark shadow in the waves behind us. The ship with no name. Abantes had found us, and he was catching up. Corpus and Castor rowed as hard as they could but they only had two oars between them and Abantes's ship had thirty. The trireme bore down on us until its prow was towering above our little fishing boat. The children screamed when they saw Abantes in his golden mask. Belos in his silver mask sniggered next to him.

The trireme bumped our boat with its keel, making it spin like a top and Abantes leaped off his ship. He landed on our deck, agile as a grasshopper. His eyes were blazing with fury.

'The ring,' he bellowed over the sound of the wind. 'Give me back my ring.'

'The ring is on its way to its rightful owner,' shouted Thrax. 'Gorgias, the merchant from New Sybaris.'

Abantes thrust out his hand. 'That ring is MINE. I am the only one in the world fit to wear it. Do you not understand?' Suddenly he made a grab for the child nearest to him – Dido. 'Give me the ring, boy, or I'll throw her into the sea.'

Dido went rigid with fear. Her eyes stared at me, wide with horror.

I dug into my bag and finding the ring held it out. 'Take it, sir. Just spare the girl her life. She is only a child.'

A look of pure triumph blazed in Abantes's eyes. He grabbed the ring from my hand and let go of Dido to slip it on to his finger. A cheer went up on the trireme and we looked up to see Abantes's myrmidons massed around the prow, their spears trained on our boat. Belos held an archer's bow with a cocked arrow. It was pointing straight at Thrax.

'We are ready for your signal, Father.'

Abantes raised the hand with the ring. I stifled a scream and a moment later I heard an angry roar behind me. Smilis careened past me like a shot out of a sling. His head rammed straight into Abantes's stomach, and they both tumbled overboard.

The waves swept them away from the boat in an instant, lifting them high on a watery mountain one moment, sweeping them down into a valley the next. I saw Smilis's thin arms battering Abantes's chest, and Abantes trying to push the slave boy under.

'The gods have mercy on them,' gasped Theopompos. 'We are very close to a deadly bit of coast here. They are being swept straight into the jaws of Charybdis.'

'Charybdis!' I cried. 'Do you mean the sea monster?'

'He means a whirlpool,' said Thrax.

Theopompos kissed his thumb in the familiar sign of fear and respect. 'This stretch of coast is famous for them. They form during bad storms and they suck anyone who comes close to them into oblivion.'

Thrax called to Fotini, who was standing by the mast. 'Throw me a rope. Nico, help me tie it round my waist. I'm going after Smilis. Hold on to the other end and please don't let go.'

'We'll do better than hold the end of the rope,' said Theopompos. 'We'll secure it to the mast. The whole ship will be holding you. If Charybdis swallows you up, we'll all come to Hades with you.'

Fotini dragged one end of the rope to Thrax and I helped tie it round his waist, cursing my hands for shaking with fear. I looped it round and round till it couldn't possibly come undone. Corpus and Castor lashed the other end to the mast.

'Good luck, the gods go with you,' I screamed as Thrax dived into the sea and the rope started slipping off the boat after him. But the wind blew my words the wrong way and I knew he didn't hear them. By now Abantes and Smilis were blurred spots in the waves, one brown, one gold. It was difficult to see through the rain but it looked like they were still locked in battle.

I don't know if it was water in my ears but suddenly the world went silent. A shaft of sunlight

pierced the clouds and everything became very sharp and clear, like a vision sent by the gods. I saw Thrax reaching Smilis and Abantes. I saw the whirlpool swirling around them, trying to drag them into its maw. I saw Thrax wrestle the slave out of the pirate's grasp. Abantes raised his dagger, his golden mask flashing in the sunbeam. And then I saw his eyes bulge with fear through the peepholes in his mask… and a moment later he vanished, sucked down into the depths by Charybdis.

Thrax and Smilis disappeared after him only a moment later. The rope went suddenly taut and I grabbed it, pulling on it with all my strength.

'Row,' Theopompos screamed behind me. 'Row, Corpus. Row, Castor. Row away from the monster.'

The rope sliced through my skin, sharp as a wet knife, as I tugged harder and harder and the salt water burned into the cuts. Still I would not stop. My best friend was at the other end of that rope, and he needed my help.

Fotini and the other children joined me and we all pulled together. Slowly the ship crawled away from the whirlpool. I kept my eyes firmly on the rope, hoping, begging the gods it would not go slack.

Thanks to the gods, it didn't. My prayers had been answered.

Fotini poked me in the back. 'I can see them, Nico.'

I looked up from the rope. She was right. I could see Thrax in the distance, Smilis still clinging to his shoulders.

We pulled them in, handspan by handspan, till Theopompos could reach out and haul them on board with his own bare hands. They both lay on the boards, gasping like fish.

Smilis held out a shaking hand to offer me something.

It was the ring of the harpies. He'd managed to snatch it back from Abantes.

CHAPTER 24

New Members for the Medusa League

'Is that why you went after the pirate, Smilis?' I said. 'For the ring?'

The boy nodded, spluttering water. 'He and Belos tricked me.'

Belos! In our attempt to save Thrax, I'd forgotten about Belos and the pirate ship hulking over us. I looked up to see if the myrmidons still had their spears trained in our direction. But the trireme had drawn back across the sea. I could see its oars dipping in and out of the water as it fought its way through the churning waves. Belos had abandoned his father when he needed him the most.

The storm died down a few hours later and we made it to the nearest harbour without any difficulty. Our little ship had taken a battering and Theopompos needed to make sure it was seaworthy before we could continue our journey to Aegina.

While Corpus and Castor were busy checking it over, Fotini and I bought food from the local agora. We shared it out amongst the children, who fell on it like a plague of locusts. After the meal, Thrax, Fotini and I found a quiet spot under the harbour wall and called a special meeting of the Medusa League. We invited Smilis and Alexa to join us.

'Smilis,' said Thrax, 'you broke the law by stealing the ring of the harpies.'

The slave boy hung his head in shame. 'I'm sorry.'

'It is not right to take other people's belongings, no matter how rich they are. Many of them worked very hard to buy their possessions. But my friends and I understand that sometimes we all do things we shouldn't. We're pushed to our limits and we take the wrong decisions. Abantes tricked you into thinking you would be able to start a new life on the high seas if you stole the ring for him. Never trust people whose promises sound too good to be true. They are almost always cheats and liars.'

Tears of remorse ran down Smilis's face and Fotini wrapped her arm round his shoulder to console him.

'But you righted the wrong that you did,' continued Thrax. 'You placed yourself in great danger to retrieve the ring from the pirate. Well done.'

He turned to Alexa. 'You have shown great courage helping us. Fotini, Thrax and I would like to thank you. Where do you come from?'

'The island of Crete,' said Alexa. 'The pirates kidnapped me while I was helping my grandfather with his fishing nets. I shall try to get back there.'

'Nico, Fotini and I have a secret society,' said Thrax. 'It's called the Medusa League because the gorgon protects us. We help people solve crime and tackle injustice, whether as a group or alone. Gaia, Fotini's slave, is also one of us. They live in Corinth. And we have a member in Delphi too. Her name is Selene. We would be honoured if you and Smilis would join us.'

The slave boy brightened up, surprised by the sudden turn in Thrax's speech and the offer to become part of our society.

'We think you are very intelligent, Smilis,' continued Thrax. 'We would welcome your help should we ever need it.'

'It would be an honour to help the great Thrax,' said Smilis. 'You saved my life and I shall be forever in your debt.' Then his face clouded over as a second thought came to him. 'But I can never go back to Aegina. Master Onatas will have me whipped for stealing the ring.'

'He has already forgiven you,' said Thrax. 'Nothing bad is going to happen to you when you get back home. I give you my word of honour.'

Smilis beamed happily.

'I will join the Medusa League too,' said Alexa. 'And if you ever come to Crete, I shall be at your service.'

Fotini pulled two medallions of the Medusa out of her bag and hung one round Smilis's neck and one round Alexa's. She had bought them at a market in the harbour. 'Welcome to the Medusa League,' she said. 'Wear your medallion always and with pride.'

Our little ceremony over, we returned to the fishing boat where Corpus and Castor were ready to sail. Aegina came into view later that afternoon and by sunset we were safely back in Inacus's house.

Gorgias and Onatas were immediately sent for, and they listened to our story with open mouths.

'My dears,' exclaimed Master Ariston when we finished. 'You put Prince Jason and his Argonauts in the shade.'

'But where is the ring of the harpies?' said Gorgias. 'I beg you, let me know it's safe.' He pulled a bulging purse from inside his chiton and thrust it into Thrax's hands. 'Here is gold for your services. I think you'll find I've been very generous.'

I reached in my bag for the ring and handed it to him. Gorgias slipped it on his finger, where it sparkled in the lamplight.

We all looked at it entranced and, once again, I marvelled at its beauty and magnificence.

But then I thought of all the people who had suffered and died because of it. Was it really worth all the pain, all the fear? I had no costly rings to wear, and probably never would. But I had things that were much more precious.

I had my parents in Kos thinking about me and offering prayers for my well-being. And I had my friends in the Medusa League, especially Thrax. He was now one step closer to buying his freedom. But perhaps best of all I had my talent – my writing. Golden rings and costly treasures don't change the world for the better, but stories do.

I was eager to sharpen my stylus and start writing about my third adventure with Thrax. I already had a title for it: *Pirates of Poseidon*.

Bonus Bits!

Glossary

Thrax and Nico use many Greek words in their third adventure. Here is a list of what they mean.

Acropolis a collection of buildings on a high hill, usually surrounded by a protective wall

Agora a marketplace, also used for public meetings

Alabastron a perfume jar, sometimes worn around the neck

Amphorae long, narrow jars made of clay, used for storing liquids

Andron a special room where men relaxed and held parties

Archon a magistrate, a very powerful and important person

Argonauts a band of legendary heroes who accompanied Jason on his quest for the golden fleece

Aulos a musical instrument made with two reed pipes

Calathus a vase-shaped wicker basket, used for storing wool and sometimes fruit

Chiton a long tunic, often made of wool

Cothurnus a laced boot of a type worn by actors and sometimes soldiers

Chytra a round cooking pot

Gorgon a female monster with snakes for hair

Gynaikon the part of a Greek house reserved for women

Hellas what the Greeks called their world

Hellenic   something that belongs to Greek culture

Himation   a long woollen garment, like a cloak, worn over the left shoulder

Hoplites   Greek citizens who also acted as soldiers

Krater   a large vase used for mixing wine and water

Kylix   a two-handled drinking cup

Kyrios   master, or lord

Lebes   a large round cooking pot, usually made of bronze

Lekythos   a long-necked storage jar

Myrmidons   a war like people. Legend has it Zeus created them from ants

Nymphs   female spirits and minor goddesses of the natural world, who lived in springs, rivers, seas and meadows

Pantheon   a group of powerful gods

Petasos   a sun hat

Pythia   the priestess of the oracle at Delphi

Rhipis   a fan, usually woven out of reeds

Stamnos   a round storage jar with two handles

Symposium   a party for men only

Tiganites   wheat pancakes, usually eaten for breakfast

Trireme   a warship with three banks of oars

Greek gods and myths

Nico mentions a lot of gods, goddesses and mythical beings in his story. Here is a list of them.

Aphaia a goddess who was only worshipped on the island of Aegina. She had a famous temple there.

Aphrodite goddess of love and beauty.

Apollo god of music and poetry.

Athena goddess of many things, including wisdom, mathematics, war and heroes. Her many symbols included the owl, the olive tree, the shield, the spear and a protective amulet with the Medusa's face on it.

Charybdis a mythical sea monster that lived under a rock in the sea. Ancient sailors believed it swallowed colossal amounts of water three times a day, which it spat out to create a deadly whirlpool.

Charon the ferryman who carried the souls of the dead to Hades, the underworld.

Demeter the goddess of the harvest and of agriculture. When the god Hades kidnapped her daughter Persephone, she abandoned the crops to look after her daughter, and the fields were destroyed by cold and rain. It was only when Zeus ordered Hades to free Persephone that Demeter brought light and growth back to the world.

Dionysus god of wine, the grape harvest, merrymaking and theatre. Many illustrations of him show him as a well-rounded old man but he is sometimes drawn as a younger person too.

Eros the god of love and friendship, often depicted as a young man with wings.

Eurus the god of the east wind. The Spartans sometimes sacrificed horses to Eurus and other wind gods. His brother Notos was the god of the south wind.

Hades the god of the underworld, which was called after him. He was also the god of the dead, and riches. His brothers were Poseidon, the god of the sea and Zeus, the chief of the gods.

Hermes god of theives, travellers and athletes, who acted as a messenger for the other gods.

Hekate goddess of witchcraft, the making of magic potions, lights and crossroads. One of the most popular goddesses in Athens, she was seen as a protector of households. Her statues often showed her holding a key or two torches.

Hephaestus the god of smithies, metalworkers, sculpture and stonemasons. He lived in the underworld, where he built weapons for the gods on Mount Olympus. He is often seen in statues holding a hammer and tongs and sometimes riding a donkey. His symbol is the volcano.

Herakles a demigod famed for his strength and his twelve feats against monsters, kings and magical creatures.

Hypnos the god of sleep who lived in the underworld with his brother Thanatos, the lord of of death. His home was a large, mysterious cave from which the river of forgetfulness flowed. It was completely silent, day and night. The entrance was overgrown with poppies.

Melinoe the goddess of ghosts. She lived in the underworld but at night, she would wander out to strike fear in people's heart. She was accompanied by a crowd of ghosts. Melinoe's body was white on one side and black on the other.

Phantasos one of the gods of dreams and nightmares called Oneiroi. Dark-winged and demon-like, they flew out of their cave in Erebos, the land of eternal darkness, to haunt people's dreams.

Poseidon god of the sea. He was also known as the earth-shaker because he could cause earth- quakes. He could create islands and springs by striking rocks with his trident.

Zeus the chief god on Mount Olympus, he ruled over the other gods with a fiery temper. His special symbols were the oak, the bull and the thunderbolt, which he loved hurling at his enemies. Zeus was married to Hera, the goddess of the home.

Acknowledgments

As always, I have a few people to thank for helping bring this book to life: Hannah Rolls, commissioning editor at Bloomsbury Education for believing in the project; my editor Susila Baybars whose tweaks and suggestions vastly improve my stories; my editor Catherine Brereton who weeded out any inconsistencies in the plot; my agent Katy Loffman who is full of boundless energy on my behalf and Freya Hartas for her wonderful illustrations.

I also need to thank Albert Schembri, a friend from the old country, with whom I discuss my ideas long before anything is committed to paper. Thank you all.